'For goodne[...]
Nicholas gritt[...]

'We all know that i[...] [...] [...] a person
for a lifetime and never get really close to them,
and yet with someone else just a short aquaintance
is enough to establish a rapport.'

There was a look in his eyes that made the defensive reply she was searching for stay out of reach,
but the resolves she'd made after her divorce
weren't going to be blown away so easily. 'The
only person I find it painless to have a rapport
with these days is myself. . .and that isn't always
as easy as it should be,' Rachel replied strongly.

He stopped in mid-stride, the light going from
his eyes, and, surprisingly, in its place she saw
uncertainty.

**Abigail Gordon** began writing some years ago at the suggestion of her sister, who is herself an established writer. She has found it an absorbing and fulfilling way of expressing herself, and feels that in the medical romance there is an opportunity to present realistically strong dramatic situations with which readers can identify. Abigail lives in a Cheshire village near Stockport, and is widowed with three grown-up sons and several grandchildren.

**Recent titles by the same author:**

RESPONDING TO TREATMENT
CRISIS FOR CASSANDRA

# OUTLOOK— PROMISING!

BY
ABIGAIL GORDON

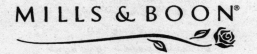

MILLS & BOON®

*MILLS & BOON and MILLS & BOON with the Rose Device
are registered trademarks of the publisher.*

*First published in Great Britain 1997
Harlequin Mills & Boon Limited,
Eton House, 18-24 Paradise Road, Richmond, Surrey TW9 1SR*

© Abigail Gordon 1997

ISBN 0 263 80122 5

*Set in Times 10 on 11 pt. by
Rowland Phototypesetting Limited
Bury St Edmunds, Suffolk*

03-9705-50685-D

*Printed and bound in Great Britain
by Mackays of Chatham PLC, Chatham*

# CHAPTER ONE

RACHEL MADDOX surveyed the clutter of her new home and wondered if it would have been better to have bought a compact modern flat instead of the stone lodge which had caught her eye when she'd spent a weekend house-hunting in the area.

She was bone- and brain-weary, but the decision was made. It was too late to be having second thoughts. She was now the owner of the house, nestling at the bottom of the drive that led to the old hall overlooking this delightful Cotswold village, and if she found herself rattling around it like a pea in a bottle she would have to put up with it.

Pushing a strand of fine chestnut hair off her face, she sank down onto the nearest packing case and looked around her, thinking flatly as she did so that it was far more fun moving into a new home when there was someone to share it with.

Her mind went back down the years to the rented flat which she and Rob had moved into when they were first married. It had been cheap and basic but they'd thought it a palace. She'd been on the lowest scale of general practice at that time—a trainee, finding her way through the jungle of a thousand ailments and going home each night to her less career-conscious young husband.

They'd been happy in those days and, no matter how tired she'd been, she'd always found the time and energy to make the most of the evenings. . .and the nights.

She and Rob had laughed a lot and played when they

got the chance, and when he'd boasted proudly to his friends that *he* had his own personal GP she had thought, in her youthful ignorance, that her russet-haired, pleasure-loving husband had been as aware of the importance of her job as she had.

That had been in the years before she'd become a junior partner in a rapidly expanding practice in a big Midlands town and—as her endless duties had taken their toll on her—Rob had become fractious, spending a lot of time with heavy-drinking acquaintances—always with the excuse that she was never there.

It had rankled that he'd seen her job as a stumbling block—that he hadn't understood the satisfaction of helping a sick person back to health, were it at all possible—and where Rob had always been eager to make up when they'd quarrelled in the early days of their marriage by that time he wouldn't stir himself to make the effort.

In the end Rachel had accepted that he was weary of the tired, pale-faced woman who had replaced the energetic medical student that he'd married, and she'd reluctantly agreed when he'd asked for a divorce.

It had been amicable enough. They were still friends, in a distant sort of way, but where Rob had been quick to make up for lost time with a string of women friends she was lonely and wretched.

Eventually, in a manner of shutting the stable door when the horse had gone, she'd decided to leave the busy city practice and had accepted a partnership in a two-doctor surgery in this village which was far enough away from Rob to make it a clean break.

The last year had sapped her spirit and vitality. She had needed every ounce of fortitude she possessed to get through the divorce, break her ties with the larger practice and move out here—but she'd done it, and was now hoping that she'd done the right thing.

'Anyone at home?' a hesitant voice asked from outside the open doorway, and Rachel got to her feet.

'I'm in here, Mike,' she called, and a second later the man who was to be her new partner came into the room.

Michael Drew was a shy, fair-skinned man with limp blond hair and gold-rimmed glasses but, during their negotiations with regard to Rachel replacing his previous partner, she had discovered that what the quiet GP lacked in social chit-chat he made up for in medical skill and dedication.

She had taken an instant liking to him which, she supposed, was fortunate in view of the fact that they would be working closely together, both in the practice and at nearby Springfield Community Hospital where they would be two of a team of GPs attending the patients there.

Rachel knew little of Mike Drew's background, except that he was unmarried, lived with elderly parents and was engaged to the daughter of a local family.

In her present state of melancholy she'd no wish to become involved in village affairs, but each time they'd met to discuss their merger she had found herself hoping that the girl was deserving of him.

'Sorry I couldn't get round to give you a hand earlier,' he said apologetically, 'but at the moment everyone for miles around seems to be suffering from one ailment or another.'

Rachel's mood was lightening at the sight of a friendly face, and she said gratefully, 'Don't apologise, Mike. It's good of you to come, but I'm sure that you have enough calls on your time already without having to help me.'

Mike was taking off his coat and rolling up his sleeves. 'Nonsense, Rachel,' he said with his diffident smile. 'It's my pleasure. I'll be easier in my mind once I know that you're settled in.'

He nodded to where the hall was visible at the end of the long drive that went past the lodge. 'I suppose you know that you're going to be in impressive company here in the grounds of Larksby Hall.' He'd picked up a packing case of kitchen equipment and, as he moved in that direction, said over his shoulder, 'Our local bigwig lives there.'

Rachel eyed him in surprise. 'No. I didn't know. Do you mean the local squire?'

He laughed. 'More like lord of the manor and that's a mild description, compared to how some folk at the Infirmary describe him.'

'The Infirmary?' she echoed.

'Yes. Nicholas Page is the top neurosurgeon in the area. He bought Larksby Hall when he moved to these parts just over a year ago.

'And so what's he like. . .this Nicholas Page?' she asked, as the realisation sank in that she'd inadvertently moved onto the doorstep of another doctor, and a consultant at that.

'Brilliant, unorthodox, impatient and, according to my normally staid receptionist, God's gift to women!' He sighed and went on with a resigned sort of envy, 'Why is it that some men have everything when it comes to charm, and I can't even manage to put a sentence together in front of an attractive woman?'

Rachel began to laugh. 'You're talking twenty to the dozen at the moment, so I can only assume that you find nothing spellbinding about me.'

The teasing comment brought the bright colour up into his neck and he said awkwardly, 'You're the nicest woman I've met in ages, Rachel. I didn't mean to be rude.'

'Of course you didn't,' she agreed softly, 'and it *is*

a long time since I looked my best, but what about your fiancée? You're obviously happy in her company, and she must be something special if you're going to marry her?'

He frowned. 'Yes, I suppose she is, but sometimes I wonder. . .' He straightened his shoulders. 'But this isn't getting you settled in. I've come to help. . .not talk your socks off.' And he set to with a determined fervour which soon transformed the clutter into only minor chaos.

It was late evening. Mike had gone, and the house had settled into quietness. They'd drunk coffee from the flask she'd brought with her and shared a packet of stale sandwiches, and now Rachel was taking fresh stock of her surroundings.

The sun was sinking on the horizon and the Cotswolds stood out blackly against an amber sky. All around her was the silence of the countryside, and she was grateful for its peace.

Later, as she stood at the bedroom window with her long chestnut hair out of its neat plait and her too-thin slenderness barely filling a cotton nightgown, the silence was broken by the sound of a noisy exhaust and, in the same second, an open-topped, white sports car zoomed through the big iron gates beside the lodge and made its way up the drive to Larksby Hall.

The lights above the gates had just come on and Rachel had seen that a dark-haired man was driving, with a woman of similar colouring beside him in the passenger seat.

She groaned softly, her tranquillity departing. *Did* she want to live in the shadow of the Infirmary's neurological genius?

'Forget him,' she told herself wearily as she turned to the hastily made-up bed and drew back the covers.

'You'll have enough to think about when you take your place beside Mike at the surgery on Monday, without worrying about your neighbours, and unless you're going to paint a red cross on the roof of this place this Nicholas Page fellow isn't going to know that he's got a humble GP nesting in the lodge.'

On that decisive note she plumped up the pillows and, easing herself thankfully back against them, she slept.

By the end of Rachel's first week in the rural practice her doubts had vanished. The charm of the house had cast its spell on her, and she was enjoying the slower pace of life in the countryside. It was a pleasure to look out of the window of her consulting-room and see trees and distant meadows, instead of tower blocks and heavy traffic.

As a working colleague Mike was ideal. He was calm and patient with those he treated, and completely helpful and informative with her.

Practising in the inner city had been hard and gruelling at times, but she was aware that it had made her into an efficient, experienced doctor and she had no qualms about coping in less fraught surroundings—even though Mike's pleasant co-operation was very acceptable.

After morning surgery on her second day they'd driven to Springfield Community Hospital where some of her time would be spent and, on arriving, he had introduced her to Ethan Lassiter, a brisk, blond man who was the hospital manager. He, in turn, had taken her on a tour of the building, explaining as he did so its function in the National Health Service scheme of things.

He'd had a special smile for a pretty dark-haired nurse in one of the wards, and as the girl had eyed him tenderly he'd said quietly, 'That is my wife, Gabriella.'

'She's very beautiful,' Rachel had told him in sincere admiration.

'Yes, she is,' he'd agreed. 'I'm a lucky man.'

His second in command, the sister-in-charge, had been just as friendly and helpful, telling her that she was Cassandra Marsland and that her husband, Bevan, was also one of the GPs who attended the patients in Springfield.

'It will be nice to have a woman doctor working with us for a change,' she'd said, 'and I do hope that you'll be happy amongst us country folk. Bevan and I live in the village at the other side of the hospital. You must come and dine with us some time.'

'That would be very nice,' Rachel had told her with a reserved smile and only a second's hesitation. She could hardly have told the pleasant, fair-haired sister that at the moment she had a yearning to be alone whenever possible because she was hurt and miserable.

It was on the Monday morning of her second week in the practice that Rachel met her prestigious neighbour, and it was a memorable meeting.

Half an hour before surgery was due to commence the door was flung open, and a dark-haired, lean tornado of a man in a smart grey suit came whizzing in.

Rachel was behind Reception, discussing with Rita— the buxom, middle-aged receptionist—a form which had been mislaid. As the two women looked up the newcomer said, 'I'm here to see Mike Drew. Is he around?'

The black leather briefcase indicated a rep from one of the pharmaceutical companies and, as Rachel looked into a pair of alert blue eyes, she said with cool pleasantness, 'We don't see salesmen until after surgery.'

'Is that so?' the newcomer said silkily. 'Thanks for the information. At what hour do you see consultants?'

Rachel stared at him. What was he on about? She was about to investigate further when Mike appeared in the doorway of his consulting-room. As the fair-skinned GP eyed him in surprise the smart stranger said crisply, 'Morning, Mike,' and, indicating Rachel, added, 'Your receptionist seems to think I'm a medical rep. Perhaps you could put her in the picture, but before you do that. . .tell me. . .who is this R. Maddox who called me out on Friday afternoon?'

At the question Rachel came out from behind the protective glass and observed him calmly. This had to be Nicholas Page. . .her nearest neighbour. . .and God's gift to women! So far *he* was the only consultant she'd asked for an appointment, and it looked as if he was under the impression that he had the licence to come barging into the practice as if he owned the place— questioning the way she did her job at the same time.

'*I* am the R. Maddox that you're enquiring about,' she told him evenly, 'but I don't think we've been introduced.'

He ran his hand through thick, dark locks and said briefly, 'Nicholas Page. . .the Infirmary,' as if the terse words were all he had time for.

'I see,' she replied coolly. 'And am I to take it that you're questioning my asking for an urgent visit to a patient? I was under the impression that the National Health Service guarantees immediate treatment for the seriously ill.'

He tutted impatiently. 'And you are right. No one is arguing about that. I was passing in the car and thought I'd like to know how the devil somebody in this place knew it was acute polyneuritis—or the jolly old ascending paralysis, as it's sometimes called? I haven't seen it that often myself.'

'I didn't *know* it was that,' Rachel said in the same level voice, 'but I was once called to a squat in

Birmingham by the police. There was a youth there who was suffering from what they thought were drug-induced symptoms but, when I had him admitted to hospital and he was seen by a neurologist, tests showed that he had the Guillain-Barré syndrome—acute polyneuritis. It was the first time I'd seen it, but the symptoms of it stayed in my mind.'

'I see,' he said in a slower, more thoughtful tone. 'Well, you were right. The patient *has* got this rare illness. Your urgency might have been a fraction overstated, but you were right to take immediate action. The condition, if not treated, can become very serious. I had her admitted to hospital immediately.' He looked around him and, turning to Mike, asked, 'What's happened to Abbotsford?'

'He's moved down south for domestic reasons,' Mike replied, 'and Rachel... Dr Maddox...is my new partner.'

Nicholas Page was looking at his watch and turning to go, but he still had something to say. 'It's fortunate that your diagnosis of patients is better than your recognition of *my* function,' he commented and, as Rachel felt her colour rise, added casually, 'And, remember, they also serve who only peddle the pills.

'So you're going to be a permanent fixture?' he went on before she could think of a reply and, when she nodded mutely, continued, 'In that case, I'll be writing to you regarding the patient in question.

'I have had electrical tests done to measure how fast the nerve impulses are being conducted, and have taken a sample of cerebrospinal fluid for analysis. Her breathing was very laboured by the time I'd had her admitted, so we've put a breathing tube in the throat.' And on that surprisingly informative note he reached for the doorhandle.

'I wish you success in your new commitment, Dr

Maddox,' he said with the same clear crispness that he applied to every word, and Rachel wondered why it seemed as if they were the only two people in the room.

'Thank you,' she murmured weakly, as she told herself that this was the way with forceful people. The power of their personality blotted out everything else.

'Whew!' Mike exclaimed when the door had closed behind the whirlwind figure. '*I'm* not geared to human volcanoes like Nicholas Page!' He smiled. 'But it's quite clear that *you* are, Rachel. You didn't bat an eyelid.'

'Why should I?' she said, still scarlet-cheeked. '*Our* functions are just as important as his. Although, in fairness, I must admit that it was a generous gesture on his part to stop by to congratulate me on picking up on the acute polyneuritis.'

'*He* can call any time he likes, as far as I'm concerned,' Rita said from behind Reception. As Rachel laughed at her fervour the impact of tall, dark vibrancy and a searching blue gaze that hadn't missed a thing about her was making her feel illogically that she was glad that her face wasn't as peaky as it had been, and that her body was beginning to fill out again after just a week in the peace and fresh air of the countryside.

It had been the previous Friday afternoon when she'd been called out to a woman in her forties who'd been in some degree of distress, with general weakness of the body and swallowing and breathing difficulties.

Rachel had been met at the door by the woman's husband, who had eyed her dubiously and said, 'We usually have Dr Abbotsford or Dr Drew.'

'Dr Abbotsford has moved to another practice,' Rachel had told him evenly, 'and Dr Drew is very busy, so you're going to have to put up with me. I'm Rachel Maddox, the new partner at the surgery, and now that I've introduced myself perhaps you'll take me to your wife.'

He reluctantly led the way to the bedroom, but there was relief in the sick woman's eyes when she'd seen that it was one of her own sex who had come to attend her.

Rachel felt that the cause of her illness might be neurological and, remembering the youth in the squat, she asked the woman if she'd had any recent throat infections.

On being told that she'd had a very painful throat a couple of weeks previously—and bearing in mind the similarity of her symptoms to those of the other patient—she immediately rang Nicholas Page's secretary to ask if he would come to see the sick woman, as she had no wish to have her admitted to hospital if *she* was overreacting.

The fact that she'd been right in her diagnosis wasn't exactly a cause for rejoicing as it meant that the patient was seriously ill, but there was some satisfaction to be had when she thought back to the reluctance of the consultant's secretary to ask him to visit the patient.

'Mr Page hasn't a vacant slot today, I'm afraid,' the girl had told her. 'He is a very busy man.'

'You appear to be misunderstanding me,' Rachel had told her inflexibly. 'We are talking about a very sick woman who needs to be seen by a neurologist. I'm sure the consultant will appreciate my sense of urgency when he sees her.'

There had been silence for a few seconds and then she'd heard, 'Five o'clock this evening is the only time I can offer.'

'That will do very nicely,' Rachel had told her and had gone back to the bedroom, where the doubtful husband had displayed more confidence in her than he'd done on her arrival.

\*     \*     \*

With the memory of a pair of vivid blue eyes still in her mind, Rachel came back from lunch just in time to take a call from Ethan Lassiter—the manager at Springfield. Mike was still on his rounds and so Rita had transferred it to her.

'We admitted one of the patients from your practice this morning,' he said, after they'd exchanged greetings. 'He was amongst the influx of Lucinda Beckman's post-operative people from the Infirmary. John Warwick is the name. He's had a hip replacement, which seems to be doing reasonably well, but he's more concerned about his waterworks than the hip. There is obviously prostate trouble and I'd like either Mike or yourself to come and look him over.'

'Yes, of course,' she said immediately. 'Mike is still out on his calls and won't have had lunch yet, but I've had mine and am free until afternoon surgery so I'll be right out.'

When she went into the hospital manager's office he eyed her slight figure in a crisp cotton blouse and tailored skirt and enquired, 'How are you settling in? I believe you've bought the lodge that used to belong to Nick Page's place?'

'Yes, I have,' she told him, her hazel eyes guarded because the conversation had taken a personal turn.

'Well, I hope that you'll be happy there. It's a delightful spot. Gabriella and I walk that way sometimes after our evening meal.'

Rachel supposed that was the moment when she should have invited them to call but she didn't, and felt churlish because of the omission. Maybe some time in the future she might feel like entertaining, but not now...not until she felt less hurt and under-valued.

The patient—John Warwick—was elderly and irritable because he was suffering from urine retention. When Rachel asked him how the hip was he barked,

'I'm not bothered about that. It's painful, but I can put up with it. What I *can't* put up with is this other problem. I'm hoping that you're going to do something about it.'

'Have you had prostate trouble before?'

'Aye, but nowhere near as bad as this,' he grumbled. 'My stomach feels swollen and painful.'

After giving the patient a rectal examination, Rachel told him, 'The prostate gland *is* enlarged, and the problem is that the bladder muscle has become over-developed due to the gland obstructing the urethra. The painful swelling of the stomach that you're experiencing is due to the fact that after a certain amount of urine retention the bladder becomes distended.

'I'm going to do a blood test and have your urine tested for infection. I'm also going to send you back, briefly, to the Infirmary—to the urology clinic—where they'll most likely do an ultrasound scan to see just how enlarged the prostate is.'

'So I'm having to be going under the knife again, am I?' he said morosely.

'Not yet awhile, Mr Warwick,' Rachel told him gently. 'You'll have to get over the hip operation first. If the prostate problem persists they will insert a catheter, which will give you immediate relief until such time as it clears up or you are fit enough for further surgery.'

As she ate her solitary meal that evening Rachel couldn't help but think about the man who lived so close to her and of their unexpected meeting earlier in the day.

She had to admit that Rita's description of him had been correct. He *was* a very attractive man—that was on the upside. On the downside, he came over as autocratic and impatient—a man who liked his own way, and was used to getting it.

She'd seen two cars going backwards and forwards to
the hall since moving into the lodge—the white sports
model, which had whizzed past in the gloaming on her
first night there, and a blue metallic Volvo—but hadn't
caught a glimpse of either driver.

The only other sign to indicate that someone was
living in the big house was when there were lights on
in the late evening. Any other indications of Nicholas
Page's domestic set-up hadn't been forthcoming.

Rachel had told herself that was fine by her, just as
long as he, or his dark-haired companion of that first
night, didn't come knocking on the door to borrow a
cup of sugar or the *TV Times*. If there was one thing
she wasn't up to at present it was being neighbourly.

It was a hot and airless night. In the middle of it,
through the open window, Rachel heard the sound of a
young child crying. Startled, she raised herself up on
the pillows and when the sound came again she got out
of bed and went to look out.

There were no other properties, apart from the hall,
for at least a mile and the distressed wailing sounded
eerie and disembodied in the stillness. Throwing on a
silk robe, she went outside and listened carefully. It was
coming from the direction of the hall, but there were
no signs of life there. The building was a solid, dark
silhouette on the horizon, and for an insane moment
Rachel wondered if someone had abandoned a child in
the bushes or something equally disturbing.

When it came again she knew that she couldn't just
keep standing there. . .she had to investigate, and she
began to walk carefully towards the stone terrace in
front of the huge pillared porch of Larksby Hall.

By the time she got there the crying had ceased and
as she stepped onto the paving of the terrace a twig
snapped beneath her feet.

'Shh!' a man's voice hissed from the shadows and

as she swung round in fright Rachel saw a tall figure, holding a small white bundle in his arms.

'I don't know who you are, wandering about at this time of night,' the same voice said, 'but for God's sake don't waken the infant—both he and I need some sleep!'

Rachel moved forward and peered into his face, and she would have been deceiving herself if she'd expressed surprise. After all, Nicholas Page *did* live at the hall. He was entitled to stroll around his own property at any time of day or night, but the last thing she'd expected to find him carrying was a chubby-cheeked infant!

'Good grief!' he exclaimed in an amazed whisper, 'it's Mike Drew's new partner! Where on earth have *you* sprung from?'

'I'm your neighbour,' Rachel told him stiffly. 'I've bought the lodge, and I'm "wandering about", as you describe it, because I was concerned when I heard the baby crying. I wondered where on earth it was coming from.'

He looked down at the sleeping child and, stifling a yawn, said, 'He's teething. I've been nursing him for hours. At least that's what it seems like. What do they give babies these days to relieve the pain?'

Rachel hid a smile. This was farcical. They were out here on the terrace at long past midnight, both of them in dressing-gowns. Her face was shiny with night cream and her hair cascaded over her shoulders in an unruly shawl, while he looked heavy-eyed and his thick, dark mop was no tidier than her own. Giving a final touch of unreality to the scene, the Infirmary's top neurologist had just asked what one gave a teething baby!

'Have you tried rubbing his gums with Bonjela?' she said solemnly, wondering what sort of mother wouldn't have been on hand to point him in the right direction, but he was giving a satisfied nod.

'That's what I've used, and it's obviously done the trick. I didn't want to disturb Felice. She's hopeless if she doesn't get a good night's sleep.'

'Aren't we all?' Rachel said drily. 'And, now that I've satisfied myself that no infant is being murdered, I'll get back to mine.'

He was eyeing her thoughtfully. 'I'd heard that a divorcee had bought the lodge, but didn't associate it with your appearance in the village practice. To tell you the truth, I'm so damned busy as the moment I never seem to surface——but that's what life is all about, isn't it?' His teeth gleamed whitely in the darkness, and the vibrancy she'd felt that morning in the surgery was there again as he said, 'Spreading oneself about.'

Rachel nodded glumly and turned to go. Apart from her career she'd felt of late that there was nothing left of her to spread, and being in the company of a man as high powered as Nicholas Page was doing nothing to make her change her mind.

'I'm sorry you were disturbed,' he said in a low voice as the child in his arms stirred in its sleep. 'The offending tooth is almost through so maybe young Toby will start sleeping through the night again for a while.'

When she got back inside Rachel made herself a mug of cocoa and, hunched in an easy chair, she went over the incredible meeting with Nicholas Page. So much for avoiding the lord of the manor, she thought. And how had he known that she was divorced? Village gossip, she supposed. It had hurt when he'd referred to her as a divorcee, but it was what she was so why be so touchy?

Maybe it was because she envied those with domestic bliss, but there couldn't have been anything very blissful in walking the darkened house with a fretful baby after a busy day at the hospital. . .and another one waiting for him tomorrow. . .while his wife slept. But, from what she'd seen of him so far, she didn't doubt that he would bounce back in the morning as fresh as a daisy.

In the middle of the following morning Rachel found Mike chatting to a girl with wispy, light brown hair and a petulant face, and when he introduced her as his fiancée, Janice Baldwin, she was hard put to hide her dismay.

At the end of a somewhat stilted conversation Rachel excused herself, on the pretext of checking a patient's records, and reeled into the small room where the files were kept, telling herself that her worst fears had been realised.

All right, she was making a snap judgement but the girl's clinging manner and tight little mouth spelt out no joy for Mike, and she thought sadly that here was a man who underestimated his attractions.

He wasn't a sparkling conversationalist, or stunning and charismatic like Nicholas Page, but there was a sincere, diffident sort of charm about him, and the last thing he needed was somebody like Janice—who had flashed a sizeable solitaire ring around like a laser while they'd been talking.

There was an out-patients' clinic at Springfield this morning, for those with problems not requiring hospitalisation yet needing minor operations or special treatments, and she was on today's rota. So—when surgery was over—Rachel pointed her faithful Fiesta in the direction of the community hospital once more.

The low, red-brick building, set in attractive gardens, was a far cry from the imposing Infirmary and the other hospitals she'd been involved with, but she was well aware that it provided a valuable service to the people in the area and that if there should ever be any suggestion of it closing because of lack of funds there would be a public outcry.

However, Mike had told her that the locals held frequent fund-raising events to help keep it open, and that they were well supported. But, he'd gone on to explain, the main reason that the hospital stayed functional was because of the excellence of its staff and administration. It had already been reaccredited twice, and when a third time came around—if the standard of care was the same—Springfield should romp home.

He had asked her if she would look in on Marianne Greer—one of his patients—while she was there, and Rachel was happy to oblige.

In her fifties, and previously a journalist on one of the daily papers, she'd had a stroke which had initially robbed her of movement down one side of her body. Now, partially recovered, the determined scribe was spending a short time in a special rehabilitation flat inside the hospital—the brainchild of Ethan Lassiter.

It was a place where patients who lived alone, as Marianne did, or were not fully ready to go back into the outside world were offered a period of residence, which acted as a transfer from the environment of the wards to normal living conditions.

Rachel found her, coping valiantly, as she moved slowly around its sunny rooms and Marianne told her, 'I'm really appreciating this time here before I go back home. I was so ill when I had the stroke that I thought I'd never be mobile again but here I am, filling the kettle, boiling an egg and rinsing my smalls, so it can't be bad, can it?'

'No, it can't,' Rachel agreed, and as she went to start the clinic in the company of Bevan Marsland— the husband of the sister-in-charge—she was full of admiration for the sanguine stroke victim and the man who'd had the foresight to make the sort of provision that she was benefiting from.

She found Bevan to be quick and very capable and, between them, they dealt with an assortment of ailments—from a bad asthma attack to a child who'd got his head stuck in the rungs of a chair.

A smart, middle-aged woman who'd fallen and hurt her hand while on holiday abroad was one of the first to present herself at the clinic, and when an X-ray showed that she had spent the last ten days with three fractures of the hand Rachel was amazed.

'I thought that because I could bend all my fingers it wasn't broken!' she exclaimed. 'Although, I suppose, the degree of pain should have told me something.'

'I think you're going to need an operation,' Rachel told the patient, to her continuing amazement, 'and for that I'm going to have to transfer you to the fracture clinic at the Infirmary.'

She was followed by an elderly man called James Wood, who was complaining of a very sore knee. When she'd inspected it Rachel said with a smile, 'Either you do a lot of praying. . .or a lot of cleaning, Mr Wood. I think you've got an inflamed bursa. You will need to have it X-rayed.'

'I don't do either,' he told her with a chuckle. 'I have a home help for the cleaning, and I leave the praying to the church folk.'

'I see,' she said mildly. 'Well, if you'd like to wait outside for a few moments I'll call you back in when I have the results of the X-ray.'

'If the bursa is inflamed it's because there is something embedded in the knee,' she was told by the radiologist from Springfield's small X-ray unit. 'It could have been there for years, and is only now causing discomfort.'

As Rachel scrutinised the plate she said, 'It looks

like a jagged piece of metal,' and when the elderly sufferer was brought back in he confirmed that he'd been wounded in the leg in the Second World War, but had been under the impression that all the shrapnel had been removed.

'Obviously not,' she told him. 'I'm going to refer you to Dr Beckman at the Infirmary. She might decide to operate to remove the foreign body.' When his mouth dropped open in dismay she said reassuringly, 'And, from what I've been told, you couldn't be in better hands.'

It was after two o'clock before she was ready to leave Springfield and as she passed the door of the general ward she saw Nicholas Page, bending over one of the beds, with Cassandra Marsland by his side.

Rachel turned away quickly. The memory of their strange encounter in the middle of the night was still vivid in her mind. Too vivid, considering that he was a man with a wife and family. Yet out there on the darkened terrace there had been no sign of the child's mother.

He'd explained that she couldn't cope with the loss of sleep but surely they both realised that disturbed nights were par for the course with young babies, especially when they were teething?

As she moved away Rachel was smiling. She was remembering his question about the Bonjela. It had made him seem less efficient. . .more human and. . .

'Dr Maddox! Have you a moment?' his voice called from inside the ward, and she knew that she'd been spotted. When she looked up he beckoned her to him, and there was nothing to do but obey.

# CHAPTER TWO

RACHEL walked slowly towards the man whom she'd last seen in a shadowed garden with a sleeping child in his arms. This was the third time that they'd met in three days. A high ratio of meetings for a GP with the same consultant.

But Nicholas Page wasn't just *any* consultant. It was obvious that he was an individualist. The fact that he'd called in at the surgery to check up on her *and* congratulate her at the same time wasn't the usual behaviour of the medical hierarchy, and his tense admission that he wasn't well informed on the treatment of teething problems wasn't the norm for a doctor either...or a modern-day father, for that matter.

There was wry amusement inside her as she thought that here was a man who could preform tricky brain surgery, without batting an eyelid, and yet a fretful toddler had him beaten.

The tousled hair and midnight stubble had gone. His shirt was as white and crisp as snow. His dark suit was a triumph of expensive tailoring, although she had the feeling that—should the occasion arise—he would wear a cloth cap and boiler suit with the same casual grace as he displayed now.

His bright glance took in everything about her as she approached, and as Rachel composed her face into a suitably grave expression for the occasion—whatever it might be—she prayed that she hadn't got a smut on her nose or a hole in her tights.

'Were you on the point of leaving, Dr Maddox?' he asked when she joined them at the bedside.

25

Rachel gave Cassandra a quick smile, before answering his question.

'Yes. The clinic is over for today.'

'I see. Only I'd like a word with you,' he said briskly. 'Might I ask you to wait for me? I'll join you outside as soon as I've given Sister instructions with regard to this patient.'

'Yes, all right,' she agreed in some surprise, and made her way into the corridor.

When Nicholas Page strode out of the ward her already quickening heartbeat began to race, and she wondered dazedly if it was this man's physical attractions or the force of his personality which were making her less calm than she wanted to be.

Whatever it was, she was acutely aware that, on very short acquaintance, he had taken her mind off her personal problems. It had needed only one glance from those startling blue eyes to make her feel like a woman again, instead of some sort of robotic nobody, and she ought to be grateful for that—if nothing else.

He pointed to the exit at the end of the corridor and suggested briefly, 'Shall we go and find our cars?'

She nodded her agreement and, matching her steps to his long stride, accompanied him onto the hospital forecourt.

Once outside he halted and, turning to face her, said, 'I'm sorry about last night. . .young Toby disturbing you. I've told his mother that her offspring's lungs have been responsible for awakening our new neighbour.'

Rachel's surprise continued unabated. Here was a very unpredictable man. Full of his own importance, yet taking the trouble to apologise for a trivial incident.

She'd been expecting him to talk shop and here he was harking back to their nocturnal encounter—the meeting which she would have imagined him thinking best forgotten.

'And what did she say to that?' she asked with a wary smile, appreciating the apology but not too happy about his taking it for granted that she'd been peeved at being disturbed.

Nicholas sighed. 'Felice can be a selfish young madam sometimes. She just popped another chocolate into her mouth and mumbled that she would mention it to Nanny when she came back this morning. It was her night off last night.'

'Motherhood *can* lie heavy sometimes, and you did say that your wife is only young. . .' Rachel said tactfully.

The comment was rewarded with an amazed snort. 'Felice isn't my wife!' he exclaimed. 'She's my sister. That little rascal last night is my nephew and, as you have just so rightly said, motherhood *does* lie heavy on her—especially as she hasn't taken the trouble to include a husband in her domestic arrangements.'

Rachel fixed him with her wide hazel gaze. So this very personable man wasn't married. That was a surprise and a pleasant one at that, if she could bring herself to admit it.

'She's a single parent?' Rachel asked, with the feeling that she ought to be on her way, instead of asking for and being given an account of the private life of her unusual neighbour. . .and his sister.

'Mmm,' he said with a frown on his lean handsome face. 'She was working as a secretary in Geneva when she started an affair with a wealthy Swiss diplomat. Little Toby was the result.'

They had reached their cars by now and, as Rachel rummaged in her bag for her keys, he answered the question which had immediately sprung into her mind.

'He already had a wife.'

'Oh, I see.'

So at least his spoilt young sister had kept the child

but, if she was as attractive as her brother, why had she needed to entice away somebody else's husband?

With a nanny in residence *and* her brother on hand she wasn't going to be faced with the hardship that many single mothers had to cope with—far from it— but the girl had still taken on a big responsibility.

With swift agility he had already slotted himself behind the wheel of his car and, rolling down the window, was about to make his farewell.

'Must dash, I'm afraid,' he told her. 'I'm in Theatre for the rest of the day.' He eyed her silently for a moment and then said surprisingly, 'Settled in, have you?'

Not quite sure which part of her new life he was referring to, she asked, 'Do you mean the job or the lodge?'

'Both.'

'Yes, on both counts,' she told him, and now there was genuine warmth in her smile. The gravity, which had seemed to be her habitual expression of late, had gone and there was a fine-boned attractiveness about her face that caught the eye.

It certainly seemed to be having that effect on Nicholas Page, if the intentness of his stare was anything to go by, but if Rachel had thought that his keen scrutiny was based on admiration she was mistaken.

'You look as if you don't eat enough,' he commented, with the sort of authority that immediately made her hackles rise.

'Really?' she remarked drily. 'You mean that I'm short of a few steak and kidney puddings or cow-heel pie and dumplings?'

Totally unabashed, he nodded. 'Maybe, or it might just be regular meals that you're lacking. *Are* you eating properly?'

With the feeling that she must be looking positively

emaciated to warrant this inquisition into her eating habits, Rachel glared at him.

'I eat as regularly as possible which is not an easy task for a doctor, as I'm sure you're aware—especially when the medic in question has been coping with the aftermath of a divorce, severing her ties with a busy city practice and settling into a new home and job... single-handed.'

She turned to go but he hadn't finished, and as he started to speak again she wondered if he'd forgotten that he'd said that he was in a hurry.

'So you've no family? Parents? Children? Friends?'

'No,' she said flatly, amazed at herself for not having sidestepped the personal discussion that she'd avoided with everyone else.

Perhaps it was because of this man's manner. The doctor questioning his patient. But *she* wasn't a patient, was she? Although she soon would be if he continued to harp on about how ghastly she looked—and just at the time when she was congratulating herself on putting back some of the weight she'd lost.

'We've got something in common, then,' he said with his bright gaze still fixed on her. '*My* parents are dead, I'm not married so I have no children and as for friends—I've a few of those, but the numbers are dwindling as they're tired of my never being available to socialise.'

'But you have your sister and the baby,' she pointed out, 'so you're not really alone.'

There was a look in his eye which told her that the relatives in question were a mixed blessing, and his next words confirmed it.

'Yes, that's correct. I have Felice and Toby, both of whom I'm very fond of, but they can be quite demanding when the mood takes them.'

'It's a fact that children can't be ignored,' she agreed,

'but when it comes to the needs of adults, well, life is what we make it, isn't it?'

Yet who was she to pontificate? The only area of *her* life that wasn't unfulfilled was her profession. Her marriage was over, her womb remained empty and—if she continued in the celibate lifestyle she had promised herself to avoid any further hurt—it would remain so. At least this idle-sounding sister of the neurosurgeon had produced a child, even though it *was* the offspring of a discarded lover.

Nicholas Page switched on the engine, and as she looked down on him the thought came into her mind that, whatever mess *her* personal life might be in and whatever wrong judgements his sister might have made, *he* certainly seemed to know what he was about and where he was going.

He had the kind of temperament which demanded and expected to be obeyed. It was in the set of his jaw, the way he held his head and in the observant blue eyes. There must be scant tranquillity at Larksby Hall with an autocratic doctor, a lively infant and its spoilt young mother. Maybe the nanny presented a calming influence. It was to be hoped so.

Unaware that Rachel was categorising his life and family, the man at the wheel of the car was ready to leave and as the vehicle moved away he said, through the open window, 'Bye for now, Rachel Maddox, divorcee of this parish.'

She eyed the departing car glacially. How dared he refer to her in such a manner? He might just as well have said 'leper of this parish', for all the difference it made. Did he think that she was one of those women who took their marriage vows lightly?

If he did he was wrong. She'd been as sincere in the promises she'd made to Rob at the altar as she'd been when she'd taken the Hippocratic oath. It was just so

tragic that the two vows hadn't been of the same importance to her husband but what was done was done and,
with the mantle of gravity back upon her, Rachel got
into her own car and drove back to prepare for afternoon
surgery.

It was half past six when she got home that evening and
as she pulled up in front of the lodge a trim, grey-haired
woman, propelling a child's pushchair, came towards
her down the drive of Larksby Hall.

They exchanged tentative smiles and, as Rachel was
putting her key in the lock, the woman said, 'You must
be Dr Maddox. I'm Meg Jardine, Toby's nanny.'

Rachel moved forward and held out her hand. 'Yes,
I am. Nice to meet you. How is the young man today?
I'm told that he's teething.'

The older woman looked down on her charge with
undisguised affection. The baby was solemnly observing a small wooden toy, clutched in his tiny fingers,
and when he looked up at them with luminous dark eyes
Rachel saw a bright red patch of colour on each cheek.

'Yes, he is indeed, poor lamb,' the nanny said, and
then added, with a quick glance at Rachel, 'I believe
that you and he are already acquainted.'

'Er. . .yes. . .we are,' she agreed reluctantly, aware
that she was becoming embroiled in the affairs of the
family at the hall again. 'I heard him crying during the
night and, not knowing there was a child living nearby,
I was concerned and went out to investigate.'

The other woman nodded. 'Yes. It was my night off.
I'd gone to stay with my sister in Gloucester and
Nicholas was left holding the baby, so to speak.'

'What about his mother? Was *she* not available?'
Rachel asked, amazed that she was concerning herself
over the welfare of a man who had enough confidence
and bounce to sort out his own affairs, without

any lukewarm championing on her part.

She sighed. 'Felice? No. She'd gone to a party at the golf club.'

'I see,' Rachel said slowly.

So Nicholas Page wasn't averse to improvising with the truth when he felt like it. So much for the sister who needed a good night's sleep. She sounded more as if she needed a good talking-to but, for heaven's sake, what had it got to do with her? All her vows of non-involvement were going to pot, and all because of a man and a baby.

'Nicholas said she came home with the milk,' the nanny informed her matter-of-factly, 'and she hasn't surfaced yet.'

Rachel's smile was wry as she did a mental comparison with what had happened during her own day. Up at six-thirty, made breakfast, showered and dressed. Took morning surgery, then made her way to Springfield and assisted Bevan Marsland with the day clinic there. Got back in time for afternoon surgery which, for some reason, was heavier than the morning one, and had now come home to cook her evening meal and maybe unwind for a couple of hours before going to her solitary bed.

She looked down at the enchanting infant and thought, with the knowledge gained from experience, that bringing a child into the world didn't automatically make a woman a mother. . .not in the true sense of the word.

It sounded as if the irresponsible Felice would have done better to take advantage of the abundance of birth-control preparations available, instead of having a child that she seemed to have little time for.

As if reading her mind, the woman whose job it was to care for him said, 'I've warned her that one day Toby will turn to me rather than her if she doesn't spend more time with him, but Felice is so difficult these days. I used to be *her* nanny years ago, and she was a little angel then.'

'And her brother? Have you always known him?' Rachel asked as curiosity overcame caution.

'No. Nicholas is Felice's *half*-brother. They both had the same father but different mothers. His mother died when he was eleven and, after a couple of years, his father married again and his new wife gave him a daughter.

'Sadly, neither of them are alive today. Only the half-brother and -sister and young Toby are left to carry on the line. Their father was a wealthy industrialist. A man with endless energy and drive.'

Who, it would seem, has passed on the same characteristics to his son, Rachel thought, but not to his daughter, from the sound of it.

The noise of a car engine on the isolated country road brought her swivelling round. The blue Volvo that Nicholas Page had been driving earlier was coming towards them, and when she saw it Rachel went scarlet.

He was here again and this time he'd caught her gossiping to a member of his household. Had he realised what they were doing? she wondered as he saluted them briefly and drove past unsmilingly.

Meg Jardine, the elderly nanny, had beamed at him in supreme unconcern, but Rachel squirmed as she asked herself what was happening to her composure.

*Nothing* has happened to it, she told herself firmly as she bade the other woman a swift goodbye.

When she'd eaten Rachel eyed the pile of medical journals she'd brought home to read. Normally she would have tackled them immediately, but tonight she couldn't settle.

She found herself wandering aimlessly around the rooms as she faced the fact that no sooner had she found herself a place to recharge her batteries than she was jeopardising it by letting another man affect her peace of mind.

This time it was not a pleasure-loving sales rep like Rob had been, but a clever, charismatic doctor who gave the impression that he hadn't much time for non-achievers.

Next morning at the surgery Mike was less than his usual equable self and when Rachel asked if anything was wrong he ran his hands distractedly through his hair and said, 'It's Janice. . .she's anxious for us to fix a date for the wedding.' His colour deepened. 'And I don't want to be rushed.'

'Good for you,' she said immediately, and Mike eyed her in surprise.

'I'm sorry,' she told him awkwardly. 'It's not for me to poke my nose into your affairs.'

'But it's what you think, isn't it?' he persisted.

By this time she was wishing that she'd kept silent but he was waiting for an answer, and so she told him in a more restrained manner, 'I've just come through a divorce, Mike. . .and it hurt. . .a lot.

'Rob and I had no doubts at all about getting married. It just seemed the right thing to do. We were that sure of each other. But because we approached maturity at different speeds our marriage landed on the scrap heap, and so my advice to you is if *you've* any doubts at all. . .wait. As you've just said. . .don't rush it. Marriage is a commitment for life or, at least, it should be.'

She was hardly going to tell Mike that the advice she was offering was partly because she'd been disappointed in his choice of partner but, then, maybe the tight-lipped Janice hadn't been exactly bowled over by her.

Rachel was spared any further expounding on caution

before marriage by Rita appearing to say that the waiting-room was full, and should she send in the first patients? When Mike told her, with obvious alacrity, to do so Rachel wondered if he wished that he'd never brought up the subject of his reluctance to marry Janice.

Feeling the need of a break, she went home at lunchtime and as she was in the middle of making a quick sandwich the doorbell rang. On answering it, she found Nicholas Page perched on the low stone wall beside her porch. As she eyed him in surprise, he said, 'Relax! I haven't come to borrow your lawnmower or a picture-hook. Can I come in?'

Her lips parted in a smile. Typical of the man, there was no 'Hello, there,' or 'How are you?' approach—just a droll announcement of his presence.

'Yes, of course,' she said with a strange feeling of expectancy inside her as she stepped back to let him in. Their previous meetings had been on neutral ground, as far as she was concerned, but today he was here in her home, breezing into her sitting-room with his usual supreme confidence.

He was looking around him appreciatively, eyeing the tasteful furnishings, her cherished prints on pale ivory walls and the vases of summer flowers on deeply recessed window-sills.

'Nice,' he murmured. 'Cool and understated, like yourself.'

Rachel's face straightened. So he'd already got her labelled as a cold fish. 'Not always, I'm afraid,' she told him with a catch in her voice. 'There are times when. . .'

Her voice trailed away. She'd been on the point of telling this disturbing new acquaintance about her miseries. She must be going crazy!

'When what. . .?' he prompted carefully.

'When I'm a mental wreck,' she told him, with the madness still in her.

'Because of the divorce?'

She turned away, not wanting to meet the searching eyes, but—still propelled by an unseen force—she murmured, 'Mmm. . .because of that. There used to be two big commitments in my life—my marriage and my job. Now there is only one.'

'So you didn't want a divorce?' he questioned flatly.

'There were times when I thought something might be salvaged out of the marriage, but basically I'd come to realise that it had turned out to be a big mistake.'

'You're better out of it if that was how you felt,' Nicholas said decisively. 'At least you weren't hurting any little ones by splitting up.' His voice faltered momentarily. 'Were you?'

'No. I have no children,' she told him levelly, with the feeling that the conversation was getting out of hand and that an explanation of his presence was overdue.

'Toby isn't ill, is he?' she asked, steering him away from her own concerns.

'No, he isn't,' he said briefly, as if he'd had to drag his thoughts back from somewhere else. 'It's Felice that I've come about.'

'Your sister?' she exclaimed.

'Yes, my sister. There's no getting through to her these days. One moment she's up in the clouds and the next she's miserable and irritable. I'm concerned that there might be a physical cause for it. . .or mental. . . and I feel that we need an outside opinion.

'Obviously I'm quite capable of treating her myself, but we're too close for me to be objective and I thought that perhaps another woman. . .'

It was his turn to stop in mid-sentence, and Rachel thought that for once he seemed unsure of himself.

'And what is it that you want of me?' she asked

warily. 'Remember, I haven't yet met Felice.'

'I want you to see her in the guise of GP,' he said promptly, back in control again. 'Take her on as a patient and see if *you* can sort her out. She's always been headstrong and wilful, but these days it's so much worse. We seem to spend all our time rowing.'

Rachel eyed the lean elegance of him thoughtfully. He was wealthy enough to send his sister to a top specialist for mental and physical appraisal, and yet he was asking *her* to get involved. Why?

'Well?' he was persisting. 'Can you see her during this afternoon's surgery?'

'Er. . .yes. . .if that's what you want,' she agreed doubtfully, 'but what makes you think she'll agree to the suggestion?'

'She has no choice,' Nicholas said firmly. 'Felice knows I'm concerned about her. . .and that I'm running out of patience. Strange as it may seem, we are very fond of each other but she knows that she can only push me so far.'

'I'll ring the surgery now,' Rachel offered, 'and ask the receptionist if I have a vacant slot for today. Can you hang on for a moment?'

'Of course,' he agreed, and at her invitation deposited himself on the couch.

When she came off the phone and informed him that she would see Felice at the beginning of afternoon surgery Nicholas got to his feet.

Having anchored her to his sister's problems, he was ready to leave and there was a nagging feeling of disappointment inside her because his visit had been prompted by a request for her services, rather than just a friendly call from a neighbour.

His direct gaze was on her and, as if reading her thoughts, he said, 'Hopefully, the next time I cross your threshold it will be for purely social reasons, and not a matter of involving you in the affairs of my family. I suppose I could have phoned with regard to Felice, but as you live so close it seemed only proper to put my request to you in person.' His voice deepened. 'And. . . Dr Maddox. . .if there is ever any way *I* can be of service to *you*, do please let me know.'

Rachel was observing the mobile mouth above a clear-cut jawline and the supple hands with their life-saving skills, and in another insane moment she thought of at least two ways in which he could be of service to her. He could awaken her dormant senses with his mouth on hers, and take the chill out of her bones with the touch of his hands.

With the realisation of where her imaginings were leading, she told him, scarlet-faced, 'Thank you, but I usually manage to cope.'

'Sure,' he said blandly, 'but the offer still stands, and now I must be on my way. The Infirmary calls.'

'Yes, of course,' she murmured, irritated now at the stilted politeness between them. . . And yet, wasn't that what she wanted. . .not getting too chummy with the neighbours?

'You'll let me know what you think about Felice?' he said from the doorway.

'Yes, I suppose so. Although there is such a thing as patient confidentiality,' she added perversely.

His eyes flashed. 'I'm aware of that!' he said touchily. 'But in this instance I am requesting the consultation as a member of the medical profession, and am therefore entitled to know your opinion.'

'You could recommend your sister to someone far higher up the medical scale than myself. So why don't you?' she said, stung by his manner and yet aware that she had provoked him.

'I think *I* am the best judge of who is the right person

to help my sister and, under present circumstances, I don't consider it to be myself.'

'And so you've chosen me!' she exclaimed with dubious incredulity. 'You haven't known me long enough to make such a judgement.'

'For goodness' sake!' he said through gritted teeth. 'We all know that it's possible to know a person for a lifetime and never get really close to them, and yet with someone else just a short acquaintance is enough to establish a rapport.'

'And you are saying that is how it is with us?' she breathed.

He shrugged. 'If you're prepared to allow it to be so...yes,' he said crisply.

There was a look in his eyes that made the defensive reply she was searching for stay out of reach, but the resolves she'd made after her divorce weren't going to be blown away so easily. As he took a step towards her, she told him with a ragged sort of purpose, 'The only person I find it painless to have a rapport with these days is myself...and that isn't always as easy as it should be.'

He stopped in mid-stride, the light going from his eyes, and, surprisingly, in its place she saw uncertainty.

Rachel was on the point of summoning her unexpected first patient of the afternoon when the door of her consulting-room opened and Mike came in, followed by a striking-looking, dark-haired girl whose extreme attractiveness was marred by the sullen droop of her mouth.

'Felice and I met outside in the car park,' he said with his easy smile, 'and we've just been getting acquainted.' Turning to his companion, he informed her, 'And now I'm going to leave you in the very capable hands of Dr Maddox.'

As he left the room Nicholas's sister managed a half-smile and seated herself listlessly across the desk from Rachel. As a momentary silence descended the two women took stock of each other.

What Rachel saw was a petulant, brown-eyed beauty who was already bored with the proceedings. What Felice Page was seeing in return she had no idea.

'Nick is fed up with me,' Felice said abruptly, breaking into the silence with brittle candour, 'and I suppose I can't blame him, but if he's expecting me to become a doting mother overnight he's due for a disappointment.'

'I think that your brother is more concerned with your discontent than your lack of motherly virtues,' Rachel pointed out mildly. 'He is worried that there might be a physical cause for it.

'I'd like to give you a thorough check-up and if all is well then perhaps we could have a chat to discover what is bothering you.'

Felice sighed. 'Whatever you say. Anything to make him happy.'

'He's very fond of you.'

'Yes, I know.' Her voice had thickened. 'If Nick hadn't been there for me during that ghastly pregnancy I don't know what I would have done.'

Rachel nodded sympathetically. Felice was very young and she *had* faced up to that.

She could find nothing wrong with her patient physically—but mentally, she wasn't so sure. Toby might be six months old but his mother was showing signs of postnatal depression.

Her hot and cold attitude towards her child and the frantic search for diversion were signs of it, and as they talked a picture emerged of an intelligent girl who'd made a mistake and, although she'd abided by it, wasn't coping with the responsibilities it had brought.

That fact, and a situation where there was no lack of money and assistance, was turning her into a sullen drone. Felice left the surgery with a prescription for antidepressants and a suggestion that she sought employment to occupy both her time and her mind.

When she'd gone Rachel sat gazing after her with the feeling that she hadn't exactly sent Nicholas's sister home with the promise of a lightning cure—it would be illuminating to hear his comments when next she saw him.

'Well?' Mike questioned when surgery was over. 'How did it go with the stunning Ms Page?'

Rachel sighed. 'I think the lady in question is a bit of a handful—difficult, unpredictable and not the most attentive mother of all time—but I feel there is a degree of postnatal depression which needs treating.'

He eyed her thoughtfully. 'In other words, she's a beautiful young thing who's made rather a hash of her life.'

'Correct,' she agreed. 'Basically, Felice is short of something to do. She should be looking after her own child, instead of fobbing him off onto a nanny. It would be understandable if she had a job but, from what I can gather from Nicholas, she either spends her time living it up or moping around.'

'What's her attitude towards the baby?'

'I've not seen her with him,' she told him, 'but I get the impression that, rather than having an aversion to the little one as is sometimes the case with postnatal depression, her problem is that she's very apprehensive about the role of motherhood, and conceals the fact behind an attitude of indifference.'

# CHAPTER THREE

RACHEL was on call that night and in the early hours she received a phone message from Springfield, asking her to visit a patient who had been taken to Casualty after a bad fall.

'She was climbing the ladder into the loft when she blacked out,' the night sister said at the other end of the phone, 'and she's either fallen very awkwardly or hit the floor with some force, as she says she can't feel her legs.

'I've told her that we'll have to transfer her to the Infirmary. In fact, I don't know why her husband didn't take her there in the first place, but she's not prepared to budge until someone from your practice has seen her. She's one of Mike Drew's patients, I believe, but he's not available tonight, is he?'

'No. It's my turn to be on duty. Mike is dining out somewhere with his fiancée,' Rachel told her, as a vision of Janice's predatory expression came to mind. 'Give me ten minutes to get dressed and I'll be on my way.'

As she got the car out Rachel's eyes strayed to the big house. It was quiet tonight, standing dark and still. No fretful wailing or footsteps pacing the terrace.

She shivered, suddenly feeling alone and vulnerable in the darkness, but it wasn't the first time she'd turned out to see a patient in the middle of the night and it wouldn't be the last. Getting behind the wheel, she drove out onto the road that ran beside the lodge.

She had barely gone a hundred yards before a car appeared from the opposite direction, and when its headlamps picked out her vehicle its driver hooted for her to stop.

Under normal circumstances it was the last thing she would ever think of doing—stopping at the request of another driver on a lonely country road in the middle of the night—but the white sports car was familiar, and the man in the driving seat clearly visible beneath its open top.

'Where are you going at this hour?' Nicholas Page asked immediately when the two cars drew level.

'Springfield,' she told him briefly, 'although I feel that your presence would be more useful than mine.'

'I doubt it,' he said tightly, 'not if it should be of the same use that it's been tonight.'

'I'm afraid I don't follow you,' Rachel said with a quick glance at her watch. Time was of the essence with regard to both the patient she was going to see and her chances of getting back to bed before the night was out, but Nicholas Page seemed uptight and very tense—and his next words told her why.

'I've just lost a patient, a guy in his thirties,' he said grimly. 'I thought we were going to hold the grim Reaper at bay, but it was not to be. He died before I could get him on the operating table.'

'What from?' she asked quietly.

'Subarachnoid haemorrhage. He was brought in a couple of weeks ago with the ballooning of an artery. It was accessible, and I'd decided to operate once the burst aneurysm in the brain had settled down enough to take the surgery. In fact, he was on tomorrow's list but, as is sometimes the case, he had a recurring attack late this evening and by the time I got to the Infirmary it was too late.'

His voice was tight with frustration. 'I don't like to lose a patient, Rachel.'

At his easy use of her first name her eyes widened.

She was aware that she liked the sound of it coming from him, although she wasn't sure why as Mike addressed her as Rachel and so did most other folk—apart from the patients.

But they weren't discussing terms of address. They were talking about something that they were both deeply involved in. . .health care. . .and, that being so, she said, 'Who does like losing a patient? But the brain is the most delicate part of the anatomy to treat, and *you* have to ply your skills in areas that are veritable minefields.

'However, I have to go. I have a patient waiting for me who needs to be transferred to the Infirmary but isn't prepared to be moved until she has seen someone from the practice, hence my being out at this hour. She has a suspected spinal injury from a fall. . .no feeling in the bottom half of the body.'

'My department, from the sound of it,' he said, throwing off his frustration. 'Lead the way and I'll follow.'

Rachel stared at him. This was taking dedication to the ultimate. 'But you've already been out most of the night!'

'So? I never sleep much, anyway. I'm too much of a coiled spring.'

No one is going to argue with that, she thought as he backed the white sports car towards the hedge and then swivelled it round into line behind her.

The night sister, a bustling, middle-aged blonde, goggled when she saw the long lean figure beside Rachel. 'It's all right, Sister,' he said calmly, 'I haven't tuned in to your thoughts. Dr Maddox and I are neighbours, and when our paths crossed half an hour ago and I heard about the patient with the spinal problem I decided that if I came along now it would be one less on my list for tomorrow.'

On that note he went striding off in the direction of

the wards and, raising her eyes heavenwards, the nurse exclaimed, 'Can we be so lucky? The great man himself, turning up at this hour! Although they do reckon that he never sleeps.'

They caught him up at the door of a small side-ward, with a young nurse hovering nervously by his side, and as the two doctors approached the woman on the bed Rachel discovered that the night was, indeed, full of surprises.

'Rita!' she said in dismay. 'I wasn't aware that you were the patient I'd been called out to see!'

The plump receptionist nodded glumly and Rachel saw that she was close to tears. 'I was getting the suit-cases down from the loft, ready for the holidays,' she choked, 'and suddenly I was falling. I couldn't stop myself, and down I went. They want to transfer me to the Infirmary, but I wanted to see Mike or yourself first to make sure that is what you'd advise.'

'I'd rather not commit myself about that until we've heard what Dr Page has to say,' Rachel said gently, aware that it was more likely to be fear of the unknown that was bothering Rita than wanting the approval of her employers.

Nicholas Page was already examining her with deft, practised hands, and after ascertaining that Rita really was experiencing complete lack of feeling in the bottom half of her body he said, 'The spine will need to be X-rayed, Sister. Fortunately that can be done here at Springfield, and from the results I'll decide if the lady needs to be moved to the Infirmary.

'I don't want her to have to make any journeys by ambulance if it's possible to treat her here. At this stage, the less movement the better until I've seen what's on the plates.'

'What about the practice?' Rita said, with tears

threatening again as she was carefully moved onto a
stretcher-trolley.

Rachel patted her hand gently. 'We'll sort something
out. That has to be the least of your worries, Rita. Just
concentrate on getting better.' She lowered her voice,
after glancing quickly at Nicholas Page—who was
straightening his shirt cuffs and making a move towards
the door.

'There's one thing that should cheer you up at least—
the Infirmary's top neurologist turning out to examine
you in the middle of the night.'

'Mmm,' she said with a trace of a smile. 'I suppose
I *am* lucky in that.'

When Rachel went to the sister's office Nicholas
Page was lounging in an easy chair, drinking coffee as
if it were the middle of the afternoon. Pointing to a tray
on the desk, he said casually, 'Help yourself. . .with
Sister's compliments.'

She eyed the coffee-pot undecidedly. 'I ought to be
getting back.'

'If you'll hang on until I've seen the X-rays we can
drive back home at the same time,' he suggested in the
same easy manner, as if his earlier tension had never
been. 'The roads are usually deserted at this time of
night so you should be safe enough, but it's not long
since one of the nurses at the Infirmary was flagged
down late at night by what she thought was an emergency and suffered a very nasty attack.'

It was pleasant to be fussed over for once but did
she want that? Their paths were crossing all too frequently for her peace of mind and so, perversely, she
said coolly, 'I've done plenty of night calls in my time.
I know how to look after myself.'

He rolled his eyes heavenwards—as if the behaviour
of lesser mortals was beyond him—and, sighing, said,
'Nevertheless, we'll do as I say,' and, leaving her

undecided whether to bow her head in subservience or repeat her previous protestations of capability, he left her to sample the coffee while he went to see if the X-ray results were ready.

'There is injury to the spinal cord,' Nicholas Page said when he came back to the sister's office. 'The vertebrae have been crushed lengthwise against each other, but at this stage it's a stable injury. I don't expect there to be any shifting of spinal bones.

'We'll keep the patient in bed for a few days to see if and what amount of movement returns to the legs. I am anticipating that there will be some. Maybe complete mobility will come back and, in that event, I will prescribe a spinal corset. However, for the present I'm afraid that it's a case of wait and see.'

Rachel's face was sombre. Rita was paying a painful price for the few seconds she'd spent teetering on the loft ladder, and she prayed that Nicholas was right... that movement would return.

As if he guessed her thoughts he said, 'I know that it's bad enough, but it could have been a hell of a lot worse. I gather from your conversation with her that the lady is the practice receptionist.'

'Yes, she is, and an excellent one too,' Rachel confirmed. 'Mike and I will have to find a speedy replacement for Rita, otherwise it will be chaos when it's time for surgery.'

'That I can well believe,' he told her as he reached across to where his jacket was slung over the back of a chair, 'and, on that thought, it's time we departed or you won't be in any fit state for coping with the ever-ailing majority.'

She gave a tired smile. It was pleasant to have someone concerned about her welfare, even if it was only on a professional basis.

For a treacherous moment she let herself imagine

how it would feel to have someone like Nicholas concerned about her permanently—to have part of his time and energy set aside for her—but she had to push the thought away before it took too firm a hold on her.

Yet she wasn't the only one who was under pressure, was she? What about him? Strong and dynamic on the outside, were there times when he needed someone to be there for *him*? With a softness in her hazel eyes, which hadn't been there before, she said, 'I imagine that you've got a full day ahead of you too?'

His eyes flickered with what could have been surprise, and his voice was gentler than before as he replied, 'Yes, I have, Rachel, so let's be on our way.'

She went to have a last quick word with Rita before they left the community hospital and found her husband seated beside the bed, anxiously clutching her hand.

'What do you think about the X-ray results, Dr Maddox?' Rita asked anxiously when she saw her.

'Mr Page has discussed them with me,' she told the stricken woman, 'and we both feel that it could have been a lot worse. Just remember, Rita, that you're in excellent hands. Nicholas Page is the best.' As the woman on the bed gave a watery smile Rachel turned to her husband.

'Are you staying with Rita? Or can I offer you a lift home?'

'I'm stayin',' he said gruffly, 'and I've got my own car here for when I decide to go, but thanks just the same, Doctor.'

When she left the side-ward Rachel found Nicholas, hovering in the corridor, and the moment they were alone he said with a slitted smile, 'I heard what you said to your receptionist, and I really don't want my capabilities trotted out as if in some PR exercise.'

'What?' she questioned blankly, realising that for

some reason he'd suddenly become touchy. 'I'm not with you.'

'I consider myself to be neither the best or the worst in my field. I just use my skills to save life whenever possible and to aid recovery.'

Rachel was tired. Until that moment she hadn't realised how tired, and anger sparked inside her. She could do without being taken to task for making what had been a completely sincere comment.

'The information was for the patient's benefit,' she flared. 'Rita is frightened and, for God's sake, who wouldn't be if they'd lost the use of their legs? I was merely trying to reassure her. I'm sorry if you don't like being discussed but, then, neither do I, and I must have been at some time or other as you'd soon sussed out that I was a ''divorcee of this parish'' —as you so tactfully described me.'

'So there *is* fire beneath all that restraint,' he said in a milder tone, as if she were the one who was being difficult.

'Yes, there is,' she slammed back, 'but at this precise moment it's not burning too well as I'm very tired, but keep on putting me in my place—like you've just done—and you might see a positive inferno!'

On that note she marched out into the deserted car park, and within seconds was driving along the road with the white sports car tagging along behind once more.

When she stopped at the lodge Rachel expected Nicholas to carry on past but he didn't. He pulled in at the side of her and, rolling the window down, said, 'I'm in no rush. I'll stay until you're safely inside.'

She turned on him wearily. 'Don't bother! I can manage!' But as she stepped up to the front door a dark shape moved out of the porch and ran across her feet. At her shout of alarm he was out of the car in a flash, and as Rachel stepped back his arms came around her from behind.

'It was a fox,' he said, as a bushy tail disappeared through the hedge.

'A fox?' she echoed. 'It almost knocked me over.'

'It would be scared. . .like you were,' he said blandly.

Rachel was acutely aware that his arms were still clasping her waist and as she twisted round to face him, ready to disentangle herself without making an issue of it, she was aware of the hardness of his chest pressing up against her breasts and his mouth only inches away from her own.

If he'd wanted to kiss her he could have done so easily and, as his eyes glinted in the light of a fitful moon, she was aware that her lips were parting ready to accept the caress, but it seemed as if Nicholas Page wasn't a man who took what was on offer.

As he released her he said, to her continuing pique, 'I overheard the old chap who tends the gardens at the hall telling Meg about our new neighbour. That you were divorced and had come from one of the inner cities. He omitted to mention that you were also going to be Mike Drew's partner and would be everywhere I turn. So, you see, *I* wasn't the one who was discussing you.'

Rachel's jaw dropped. Was he accusing her of pursuing him? Couldn't the man see that she wanted to be left alone? She might have weakened for a few seconds when she'd been in his arms because it was so long since she'd been that close to an attractive member of the opposite sex—and it *was* blood that ran through her veins—but she was rallying.

'I see,' she said coolly, 'and now that you've justified yourself I'll say goodnight.' Without more ado, she opened the door and made to go inside but he caught her arm and pulled her back.

As she swung round to face him, he said smoothly, 'We've been together for most of the night and during that time I haven't had the chance to talk to you about Felice.

'I know it's late and you're tired, but you sent her home with a prescription for antidepressants, for God's sake...and the suggestion that she seek some sort of employment. Was that the best you could do?'

She glared at him. 'Yes, under the circumstances, and I didn't prescribe the antidepressants for the fun of it...so that I might be *seen* to be treating her! My opinion is that she's suffering from some degree of postnatal depression, and my suggestion regarding a job was therapeutic. She has too much time on her hands, both for pleasure and moping around.'

Nicholas took a deep breath. 'So there is nothing physically wrong?'

'Not that I can see. It's clear that the pregnancy had a traumatic effect on her, and only time will make the memory fade. If you're not happy with my findings I suggest that you do what I recommended in the first place...consult someone else. Or treat her yourself!' On that dismissive note, she went inside and this time he didn't try to stop her.

When Rachel informed Mike of Rita's accident the next morning his reaction was typical of him. His concern about the running of the practice during her absence came second to his concern for the injured receptionist, but he still had to face the practicalities of the situation.

'We're going to need a temp with all speed,' he commented as they eyed the empty space behind reception. His face became thoughtful. 'I wonder...?'

'Wonder what?' she asked curiously.

'It would depend on whether you were in agreement, though,' he went on, without answering her question.

'I can't tell you if I agree until you explain what you're talking about,' she said with a smile.

'Yes, of course,' he agreed musingly. 'It's just an idea, but it might work.'

'Mike!' she said laughingly. 'Are you going to tell me or not?'

'Felice Page,' he said. 'She's smart, intelligent and would benefit from some kind of occupation. How about us asking her to fill in during Rita's absence?'

Rachel's eyes widened. Was he crazy? Suggesting that they had the chocolate-gorging, party-pooping, lukewarm mother hold the fort in Reception?

He was eyeing her questioningly. 'What do you think, Rachel?'

She knew what she thought. It would be a disaster unless Felice Page was an administrative wizard with a deep fount of knowledge about health care. But, strangely, Mike didn't seem to feel that way, and it was the first thing that they hadn't seen eye to eye on since she'd joined the practice.

'I could ask Brenda Starkey to come in for a few days to show her the ropes,' Mike was saying. 'She worked here for years until retiring eighteen months ago.'

Rachel sensed a determination in him that she'd not witnessed before, but Mike wasn't aware of her yearning for privacy and she felt that if she agreed to his proposal she would be allowing the man from the hall even more into her life. For, if his sister was employed at the practice, she was certain to see more of him than she was doing already, and she was having a job to cope with *that*.

However, her partner did have a point. They needed a receptionist badly, and if he thought that the Page girl could do it she might as well fall into line.

'Go ahead, if that's what you want,' she said levelly,

'but don't blame me, Mike, if she turns out to be absolutely useless.'

'Steady on,' he said with his quizzical smile. 'I haven't asked her yet, and when I do it will be a good test of whether she really is bone-idle or not. I'll speak to her right away.'

When Mike came out of his consulting-room he was smiling. 'She'll do it. Didn't bat an eyelid. I've explained that there'll be someone here to show her our system. . .and guess what she said?'

'I don't know. What?'

'That it wasn't necessary. That her brother is a doctor and she has been a private secretary.'

'Cocky young madam!' Rachel exploded. 'Let's hope that she knows what an enema is—and that when old Emma Royd comes in to see you that she doesn't call out her name as if referring to an aggravated form of piles! When can she start?'

'She'll be here shortly and, in the meantime, I'll see if I can get hold of Brenda.'

'So you're not going to take Felice Page at her word and let her cope alone?'

He smiled. 'I'm not *that* optimistic, Rachel. It takes some doing to hold the fort in a busy surgery. Our new recruit could have second thoughts when she sees what's involved.'

Rachel was gazing out of the window, her thoughts veering to another member of the Page family—the man who was as thoughtful as a lover one minute and as prickly as a hedgehog the next.

As the memory of the time they'd spent together in the small hours of that same morning surfaced with disturbing clarity, she wondered what his reaction would be to his sister being employed in the village surgery.

She was soon to find out. Brother and sister arrived

in their respective cars shortly after elderly Brenda Starkey had presented herself. Because Rachel's curiosity with regard to Felice Page had been appeased, it was at Nicholas that she looked first and was regarded in return with a cool, measuring glance which brought back the sensations of their recent parting.

It only rested on her for a second, and then he was saying to Mike, 'Top marks for effort, Mike. Anyone who can get my sister out and about at this time of the day is no mean performer.'

Felice Page was looking around her, and where her brother's face was surely the mirror of his mind hers was expressionless. Rachel prayed that this idea of Mike's wasn't going to throw their orderly practice into confusion.

'Let me show you round, Felice,' Mike said with an easy smile, as if to counteract her own anxiety, and as he took her through the now-empty waiting-room Rachel was left alone with Nicholas.

'And how are *you* this morning?' he asked. 'Sleepless and stunned?'

Her smile was pinched around the edges. 'Sleepless, yes. I'm not quite sure what you mean by ''stunned''.'

'I'm not harking back to the fact that you remembered you were a woman for a few fleeting seconds last night,' he said with an enigmatic smile of his own. 'I'm referring to your having another member of the Page family intruding into the privacy that you guard so keenly.'

Her colour had risen at his reference to the way she'd reacted when he'd held her in his arms the night before, but she covered her embarrassment by parrying back, 'You appear to read my mind very accurately.'

He was observing her thoughtfully. 'I've met a few divorced people in my time and I find that they either live it up when they gain their freedom. . .or shrink into their shells.'

'And you've got me down as the shrink-into-shell type?'

'I'm not quite sure what type you are, but you certainly don't seem to be living it up.'

'Chance would be a fine thing,' Rachel told him with a dry laugh. 'There aren't enough hours in the day at the moment but, having said that, I don't make a habit of going home to a bowl of gruel and my embroidery.'

He ignored the sarcasm. 'You need to get to know the locals.'

'Is that what you did when you moved here?'

'Er. . .no. I've never had the time.'

'But you think I have?'

He ignored the question and said, 'Felice tells me that the Friends of Springfield Hospital are holding a fashion show in the town hall on Friday night, and there's a cricket match being played on the village green on Saturday. Those are two events where you could get to know people.'

Her amazement was increasing. Was this high-powered Adonis trying to organise her social life too? He'd already held an inquest into her eating habits. It was fortunate that she wasn't on the lookout for a new relationship. Checking up on her calories and fobbing her off onto the villagers to pep up the small amount of spare time that she hadn't even begun to plan for was hardly going to be the gateway to romance.

But there was no way that she wanted he of the keen eyes and laser-like mind to guess the extent of her surmises about him, and so she asked casually, 'And will you be taking part in the cricket match?'

She didn't expect for one moment that he would be— the lord of the manor, and whiz-kid neurosurgeon to boot, mixing with the locals.

His eye was on the gold watch on his lean brown wrist and she sensed that he was on the point of leaving, yet he answered the question in a leisurely enough manner. 'Yes, circumstances permitting. Ethan Lassiter has asked me to be on Springfield's team. It's hospital against villagers, and as I have a sincere regard for the work that the small community hospital does in the neighbourhood I like to support it when I can.

'Apart from anything else, Springfield needs the money that events such as these bring in to help it to stay functional. The villagers and the staff at the hospital are aware of it and work unceasingly to that end.'

His gaze shifted upwards to where Mike and his sister were moving about in the rooms above, and he said in a low voice, 'I wasn't questioning your judgement last night when we discussed Felice.'

'No?' she queried dubiously.

'No,' he assured her. 'It was just a matter of my being blinkered when it comes to my sister. I've looked after her for so long that it is hard to make an impartial judgement, and I see so many serious illnesses of the mind in my profession.'

'I would have thought that postnatal depression is complicated enough, but I get your point. It's so difficult to get things in perspective when the person is a member of one's own family. One's own expertise seems as nothing when the problem is so close to home,' Rachel told him with generous sympathy.

'But I really do feel that all Felice's problems stem from having Toby—and perhaps too easy a lifestyle—and that once those two things have been dealt with she will be fine.'

'The tablets should help with the depression. . .and Mike is hoping that offering Felice a job here will solve her other problem *and* our staffing difficulties at the same time.'

Nicholas reached out and touched her cheek. It was just a fleeting salute but it felt like a caress and for a wild moment she wanted to reach out for his hand and hold it there, but she could hear voices. Mike and Felice were coming back to join them, and as they drew nearer Nicholas murmured, 'You said a few moments ago that I read your mind.'

She nodded, still mesmerised by the moment. 'Well, maybe I do,' he said slowly, 'but you've just done the same thing for me. You've understood how I felt about Felice.'

Rachel's heartbeat quickened. Nicholas had said that there could be a rapport between them. . .if she would allow it. And that was what she was doing, letting this chemistry between them take hold of her, but before she could tighten her hold on the moment Mike and Felice were upon them and Nicholas was saying in his usual brisk manner, 'Well? Are you going to do your bit for health care, Felice?'

'Yes,' she said quickly, her eyes on the fair-haired man at her side. 'It will do for starters.'

Rachel felt irritation rise inside her. Nicholas might come over as a bit high-handed, yet he had the right to be so if he wished—but this young madam!

He was frowning and she sensed that she wasn't the only one to be irritated by Felice's manner when he said, 'Working here for Mike and Rachel will help to relieve the boredom that you're always complaining of, Felice, and maybe the motivation you get from this job will increase your interest in young Toby. Now I must go. Fortunately, I only have an afternoon clinic today.'

As he made to depart he said, with his bright, mesmeric glance on Rachel, 'Maybe I'll see you at the cricket match, then, Dr Maddox?' To Mike, who appeared to be the only one who wasn't riled by the youthful arrogance of the girl beside him, he added, 'I've been trying to get your partner interested in village life, Mike.'

On that note of explanation he left, and with his going the summer sun streaming through the surgery windows seemed less bright and the day ahead not quite so challenging.

Rachel left Mike and the elderly Brenda to show Felice the surgery routine, and made her way to Springfield to see a patient whom she'd had admitted with a varicose ulcer.

As she approached the small red-brick hospital, with its bright paintwork and colourful gardens, she was aware—as she had been on other occasions—of how attractive it was, compared to the dark stone façade of the Infirmary.

Springfield was a cosy place in which to recover from surgery or to be hospitalised for a minor complaint, and the members of its staff she'd met so far had been pleasant and extremely helpful.

Ethan Lassiter's brisk competence reminded her to a lesser degree of the man who had been cataloguing the social life of the village for her earlier that morning, and the hospital manager's beautiful young wife— to whom she'd spoken on a couple of occasions— appeared to combine her nursing skills with an appealing sense of humour.

She had taken an instant liking to his assistant, Cassandra Marsland, and found her husband, Bevan, just as easy to get on with and as dedicated as his wife in caring for the folk in the small community hospital.

The patient, a middle-aged shop assistant, had suffered from varicose veins in her legs for some time and when eventually the skin of her legs had become thin and dry it had broken and formed a painful ulcer.

'A doctor from the Infirmary saw me this morning,' she said the moment Rachel appeared beside her in the day-room, 'and he says that my veins need stripping.'

'Yes, they do,' she agreed, 'and he will do it for you here. It isn't a long operation.'

'What exactly does it entail?' the woman asked. 'Only I can't be off my feet for too long as we need my wages, and because I've always worked as a temp I don't get sick pay.'

'You won't be off your feet,' Rachel reassured her. 'In fact, it will be just the opposite. You will be encouraged to walk as much as possible.

'The operation consists of an incision in your leg to expose the greater saphenous vein and its main branches. The vein is then clamped and cut and the ends securely tied. The branches receive the same treatment.

'A length of wire with an arrow-shaped metal head will then be passed downwards through your leg with the vein secured to it, and when the higher opening has been closed the wire will be withdrawn through a smaller incision lower down the limb.

'As the wire, or stripper as it is called, comes out it will bring the vein which has bunched up in the process with it and the protruding branches will fall away.'

There was the usual apprehension in the patient's eyes and Rachel told her gently, 'It's a minor operation that is done all the time, and once you're over it you'll appreciate the benefit.'

She called at the sister-in-charge's office on her way out, and when Cassandra looked up and saw her framed in the doorway her smile flashed out.

'I came to ask if you have any tickets for the fashion show,' Rachel said with an answering smile. 'Or do I have to contact the Friends of Springfield?'

The blonde sister opened a drawer in her desk and produced a pile of stiff cardboard squares. 'No, I have some here,' she said. 'How many do you want?'

'Just the one.'

'If you're going to be on your own why not join

Gabriella and myself and my friend, Joan, who used to be matron-manager here? We're all going and you'd be very welcome to make it a foursome, Rachel.'

She was wishing that she hadn't mentioned the ticket if she was going to be involved in a 'girls' night out', but Nicholas's casual comment had reminded her that it was ages since she'd bought any clothes. Maybe that had been behind the suggestion—that he'd thought she could do with smartening up. If he had, he was right.

Of late she'd behaved like a frump, thought like a frump and dressed like a frump. If she'd died they would probably have buried her in a cotton shirt and a skirt in place of a shroud, and on the crest of that wave of self-criticism she gave in and said, 'Thank you, I'd like to join you.'

And why not? the voice of reason said. You have to admit that since you moved to this delightful Cotswold village life hasn't seemed so empty, and there could be various reasons why. Such as the peace and freshness of the countryside, this caring hospital tucked away beside the fast-flowing river. . .and last, but by no means the least, making the acquaintance of a man who is so opposite to Rob in every way it just isn't true.

Beside Nicholas Page, her extrovert ex-husband seemed like a study in still life. With regard to herself, *she* felt like a pale shell in his presence and now there would be his confident young sister, presiding over Reception at the surgery once Brenda had explained the routine.

As she went to find her car Rachel found herself smiling. At least he wouldn't be at the fashion show. That was one occasion when he wouldn't be there to confuse her.

Felice was presiding over Reception when Rachel turned up for afternoon surgery, and she had to admit

that for a new broom she was coping admirably. Perhaps
not as chatty and sympathetic as Rita, but dealing with
old and young alike with swift efficiency.

Observing her, Rachel thought, here is a lukewarm
mother with a beautiful child. Why doesn't she spend
more time with her baby? Maybe she would if Nicholas
and the nanny weren't there to support her but, instead,
Mike was offering her a temporary escape from the role
which sat so lightly on her shoulders, and she hoped
that he knew what he was doing.

In a quiet moment she asked perversely, 'How is
Toby? Any more teeth?'

Felice was getting out a patient's files, and she swung
round quickly. 'He's fine,' she said abruptly. 'The one
that was bothering him the other night is through.'

'Good,' Rachel said evenly. 'That must be better for
*all* of you.' But the girl wasn't listening. Her eyes were
fixed on someone else. Mike had been called out to an
urgent case in the middle of surgery and had just got
back. He was standing in the doorway, the tolerant
eyes behind gold-rimmed glasses observing them both
warmly, and as her glance switched back to their new
receptionist she saw that Felice's mouth had lost its
downward curve.

# CHAPTER FOUR

ON THE night of the fashion show Rachel was late getting home. Afternoon surgery had been long and taxing, and just as she'd been about to leave a call had come through for an urgent visit to a patient with Crohn's disease.

She'd had to arrange admission to the Infirmary for a very sick man for the draining of a suspected abscess in his stomach, and had stayed with the distressed patient until the ambulance came.

By the time she'd driven home and had her evening meal any inclination to get ready to go out was dwindling fast. But, in Rachel's book, a promise was a promise—be it large or small—and so on that premise she showered, changed, and sallied forth, leaving the village behind.

The main building of the elegant Midlands town was ablaze with light when she got there and the car park was almost full, but she managed to find a space. As she hurried up the flight of stone steps leading to the town hall the tall figure of a man came down towards her, his face in shadow but the lithe grace of him unmistakable.

What was Nicholas doing here? she thought in the split second before they drew level. She'd already told herself that this certainly wouldn't be his scene, and yet here he was.

'So you're taking my advice and entering into the social life of the area?' he said, as if she were a patient that he'd had to prescribe for. '*I'm* here merely as chauffeur.'

'Ah, I see. You've brought Felice.'

'Wrong. Felice, for once, is minding her own child. I've brought Meg. She's meeting one of her cronies here.'

He looked her up and down in the light from the huge windows of the building, and said surprisingly, 'Cast off your divorcee's weeds, Rachel. Buy something beautiful while you're here. . .in peach or jade to offset that self-imposed pallor and the amazing chestnut hair.'

Her heart skipped a beat. He actually sounded as if he meant it and for a wild moment she hoped that he did, but those sorts of feelings were against everything she'd vowed to be free of. Was she going to be organised like this every time she saw the man? Told what to eat? Where to go? What to wear?

'I'll bear your comments in mind,' she told him with cool irony, 'although I've never seen myself as a bird of plumage.'

'There's a first time for everything,' he replied, unperturbed.

The conversation was becoming too personal, she decided, and with a swift change of topic she said, 'I'll give Toby's nanny a lift home, if you like. It will save you having to turn out again.'

'I wasn't intending to,' he informed her. 'She was going to get a taxi back, but I'm sure she will be grateful of the offer of a lift. I have a dinner engagement and therefore am not available to take her back, so as you live practically on our doorstep. . .'

'Indeed I do,' she retorted calmly, and could have told him that she frequently wished she didn't. 'I'll look her up in the interval and tell her that I'm taking her home.'

'Yes, if you would, and now I must be off or my dinner guest will be thinking I've stood her up.' With a casual wave of his hand, he was gone.

So much for that, Rachel thought as she made her way through the crowded foyer. It sounded as if there was nothing wrong with *his* social life. The tale about his friends drifting away because he was never available didn't seem so convincing at this moment. But that might be because she was curious. . .and peeved because he'd merely recommended a night out at a fashion show for her, or an afternoon on the village green, and certainly not wining and dining. . .with him!

She sighed. But she didn't want that, in any case, so why whinge about it?

Rachel enjoyed the evening much more than she'd expected. It was pleasant to be in the company of her own sex—with honey-blonde Cassandra, dark, bubbly Gabriella and Cassandra's friend, Joan Jarvis, who was plump, middle-aged and enjoying unexpected motherhood.

As the former matron-manager of Springfield rhapsodised about her young son during the evening Rachel found herself comparing her with Felice, and it was easy to see which of the two women's behaviour was the more normal.

It was with Nicholas's sister and her child in mind that she sought out Meg Jardine in the interval and offered her the lift home. Once the nanny had quickly fallen in with the suggestion, Rachel went back to join the others.

'What have you done about replacing Rita?' Cassandra asked as they made their way back to their seats.

'Brought in a raw recruit,' Rachel told her.

'Who?'

'Nicholas Page's sister.'

'Our sizzling neurosurgeon has a sister? What's she like?' Joan Jarvis asked.

'Extremely attractive and very confident,' she told her.

'She takes after him, then,' Gabriella said, and with her dark eyes dancing, added, 'If I wasn't so madly in love with my husband I'd get a transfer to the Infirmary.'

'I could see Ethan letting you do that!' Cassandra chortled as the models appeared once more on the catwalk.

When the show was over those present were given the opportunity to try on any garments which might have caught their eye and, because she had gone there specifically to give her wardrobe a new look, Rachel joined them.

As she looked along the rails of fashionable clothes she could hear in her mind the cool voice of authority telling her what to buy. Almost as if Nicholas Page was controlling the moment from a distance, she saw an evening gown made out of jade-green satin.

It was long and slinky. Not the kind of creation one would choose if out for the evening with the Michael Drews of the world or with a man like hard-drinking, pleasure-loving Rob, but a woman wearing it would be the perfect foil for a tall, decisive neurosurgeon who made heads turn wherever he went.

Inside a cubicle Rachel surveyed herself in the mirror. The dress transformed her. It turned the neat, pale-faced doctor into a very desirable woman, and as her lips parted in pleasure and her hazel eyes glowed she swung her silky brown mane from side to side.

She was in thrall, but only for a crazy moment, then she was berating herself for being so malleable, and she unzipped it and put it back on the hanger—turning her attention to a couple of smart suits which had caught her eye.

Gabriella was at the counter as Rachel went to pay

for the suits and she asked, 'How did the gorgeous green creation look?'

'Lovely,' she said quietly, 'but I couldn't foresee an opportunity presenting itself for me to wear a dress like that.'

'Sometimes the fact of having the right clothes creates the opportunity to wear them,' Ethan's young wife said as the assistant placed the white evening gown she'd just purchased into a trendy carrier bag.

Maybe, Rachel thought, but her present lifestyle did diminish the possibility somewhat.

Listening to Meg Jardine's chatter on the way home, it would have been easy for Rachel to have brought Nicholas's name into the conversation. If she mentioned their meeting on the town hall steps the nanny would almost certainly volunteer details of where he'd spent his evening.

The same applied to Felice. To say her name could bring forth information as to how she liked the job — if it was helping her to sort out her attitude to life in general and Toby in particular, and maybe what the girl thought about Mike and herself. But she and Nicholas had already crossed swords with regard to their combined distaste for gossip, and so she kept silent.

Not so her companion, however. She was full of praise for what she saw as Mike's clever therapy in getting Felice to do something useful. With a homespun kind of wisdom, the elderly nanny remarked that with her mind more occupied Nicholas's sister might stop dwelling on the pregnancy which had disrupted her life and get her future into perspective.

'Nicholas has always looked out for her,' she went on, 'but even he has been affected by her moods of late, and yet it isn't Felice's fault, is it? Before she had Toby the girl never knew the meaning of discomfort.

'I thought that Nick would have treated her himself. Like you, he thought her problem was postnatal depression—or even something worse—but I imagine that the arrival of a sympathetic woman GP in the village gave him the opportunity to bring in someone less involved with Felice.'

As if tuning in to Rachel's curiosity about his movements during the evening, Meg said obligingly, 'He's out with an old girlfriend tonight. I do hope that he enjoys the occasion as he gets so little free time, but I knew that when Gaynor Kingsley came on the scene again he would make the effort to see her somehow.'

So the human dynamo was out with an old girlfriend...and why not, for heaven's sake? What Nick Page did with his life was no concern of hers, Rachel decided as she garaged the car, and so why did she lie sleepless in her bed after a long, exhausting day?

Eventually she got out of bed and went to stand by the window. 'It isn't working,' she told herself. 'You can't shut out your desires...your senses...to order.' But then the memory of Rob's casual treatment of her came back to mind, and she knew that she could...she had to if she was to stay sane.

Her eyes strayed to the dark bulk of the hall on the dawn skyline. Was Nicholas asleep in one of its stately bedrooms, or was he elsewhere and maybe not sleeping at all?

The second fund-raising event that weekend in aid of Springfield Hospital was a much less glitzy affair than the fashion show. The lush green of what was to serve as the cricket pitch was in sharp contrast to the mulberry velvet drapes of the catwalk, and those seated on rough wooden benches around its perimeter weren't interested in clothes. They were out to spend a leisurely afternoon in the sun, and were dressed accordingly.

Rachel had done likewise. In a lemon cotton shift and open sandals—and with her hair in its usual smooth chestnut plait—she was feeling back on form.

With her mental meanderings of the night before put firmly to the back of her mind, she'd decided that she was going to obey the oracle once more and get to know the people of the village—those she hadn't already met in the surgery.

All her new acquaintances from Springfield were there and she espied Felice behind Toby's pushchair, with Meg Jardine at her side. Mike was also on view, with Janice glued to him like a limpet, and as always when she saw the two together there was a sinking feeling inside her.

Janice's amiable partner must be blind if he couldn't see what he was letting himself in for but, as she'd once said to him, who was she to criticise another person's relationship when she hadn't been able to handle her own?

The only person she hadn't seen so far was Nicholas, and until she did Rachel knew that the reality of her new resolve wouldn't be there.

She needed a dose of his brisk impersonality to strengthen it but, typical of his ability to confuse her, when he came strolling across to where she was sitting—his cricketing whites dazzling in the sun—there was a look in his eyes that made her go warm.

'So you've taken my advice and come out of your celibate cell?' he said with a satisfied smile.

'I was too frightened to do anything other than obey,' she told him with mock temerity.

That brought amusement to the face which was never out of her mind, but he didn't take her up on it. Instead, he asked in his usual brisk style, 'How is Felice settling in at the surgery?'

'It's early days yet,' Rachel told him, 'but I—who,

I must confess, wasn't keen on the idea—am having to have a rethink, as she appears to be coping very well for someone who had no previous knowledge of the workings of a general practice.'

He gave a satisfied nod. 'It's good to hear that. As our parents are no longer alive I feel responsible for Felice and Toby, although it's a responsibility that I sometimes feel I could do without. But blood is thicker than water and, added to that, I don't like messy situations.'

She gave a rueful smile. 'Mine won't appeal to you, then. A divorcee with a personal life that is as empty and disorganised as it possibly could be. I'm on top of my job and like to think I always have been, but the rest of it. . .'

As soon as the words had left her mouth Rachel could have bitten them back. He would think that she was asking for pity, and that was the last thing she wanted. What she *did* want was to be left alone and so why, for heaven's sake, was she here, mixing with the locals and bringing herself under the keen scrutiny of Nicholas Page once more?

'I can suggest therapy for that problem,' he said in a less forceful manner than he normally used. 'It's what they call the sleeping beauty technique.'

Rachel's face coloured. He was making fun of her.

'If you'd like to accompany me to where I've parked my car I'll explain what I mean.'

She stared at him. This guy was something else. Couldn't he forget that he was a medical man for five minutes? What sort of therapy was he carrying around with him, for goodness' sake? And what a nerve to suggest that she needed it!

All was about to be revealed. Nicholas had parked his car in a small wooded area at the bottom of the lane leading to the village green, and when they reached the

blue Volvo Rachel stood stiffly beside him as she waited
for him to unlock it and bring forth details of the medication he'd suggested.

Instead he turned to face her, and with her hazel eyes
wary and defensive she said, 'And so what is it that
you're going to prescribe this time? We've had the
nourishing food lecture, and I've been told the colours
I should wear. I've turned up at a gathering of locals,
as you recommended, and now you're offering to pep
up my mental processes. Can I be so lucky?'

'It's not your mental processes I'm offering to treat,
Rachel,' he said softly. 'This is the kind of therapy I
had in mind.' As the realisation of what he meant began
to dawn on her she stiffened, but it was to no avail.
Nicholas reached out for her and pulled her towards
him, and as his arms came around her and his lips sought
hers he murmured, 'I never could resist a challenge.'

Mesmerised by his nearness, Rachel heard what he
said but it didn't immediately register because now he
was kissing her and, after the first few seconds, she was
responding with a fervour that she would never have
believed possible—her head thrown back, her breasts
stiffening and her thighs aching. In the middle of the
unbelievable moment of passion came the realisation
that what she'd had with Rob had never been like this.

Or was she thinking that because it was so long since
she'd been found desirable, kissable? As the embrace
went on and on she didn't care. Whatever Nicholas
Page suggested she did seemed to be right, especially
this course of treatment he was prescribing!

But was that what it was to him—an experiment in
thawing out frigidity? She stiffened in his arms. What
was it he'd said just before he kissed her? That he never
could resist a challenge?

Aware of her sudden stillness, he released her mouth
and, lifting his head, he looked down onto her pinched

face. 'What is it?' he asked. 'What's wrong?'

'I'm just an experiment to you, aren't I? You've just said you can't resist a challenge. The great Nicholas Page, who's used to dealing with head cases, thinks he'll have a go at sorting out the frustrations of a cold fish GP.

'Well, I've got news for you. If there is any healing to do I will do it myself. They've just announced over the loudspeaker that the match is about to start, so it would appear that your presence is required by those who really *do* need you.'

As she went back to join the crowd who'd come to watch the cricket Rachel was seething, and most of her anger was directed at herself. She'd behaved like a gullible teenager out there in the wooded clearing with Nicholas Page, and it wasn't going to happen again.

But she knew that the memory of his mouth on hers, his arms around her and the feeling that they were as of one blood wasn't going to be easy to wipe out of her mind. Not wanting to face him again so soon, she decided to go home.

However, at that moment she was waylaid by Cassandra and Gabriella, who informed her that both their husbands were playing on Springfield's team and would she like to join the deserted wives' consortium?

Thinking grimly that the term described her exactly, she reluctantly agreed to sit with them and was introduced to the wives of the two porters, who were also on the team.

Gary, the youngest of the two men, was the father of a small girl, and when he appeared as the opening bat the little one clapped and waved delightedly.

As the sunny afternoon dawdled on Rachel began to calm down. Forget what happened, she told herself, because the more you think of it the more you'll have to admit that you enjoyed it—that you would have craved for more if you hadn't found a shred of common sense to save your dignity.

Amidst the satisfactory sound of bat hitting ball and the occasional cry of 'Howzat?', the group of them sitting together took turns to go to the tea-tent for refreshments. All in all, she would have thought it an idyllic afternoon—if only she could have forgotten those moments with Nicholas.

When the first side were out and the interval was announced Rachel braced herself to face him again if he should come across to where they were sitting, but he didn't. Instead, he went to sit with Felice and Meg Jardine, and as he did so she breathed a sigh of relief.

At the end of the match Cassandra said, 'We're all going to The Goose for a meal. Would you like to come along, Rachel?'

She hesitated. Did she want to go? Not particularly, but, then again, did she want to go home and prepare herself a lonely meal? The answer to that was no once more.

It *was* nice to be socialising with other people again, she admitted to herself, just as it had been last night at the fashion show, and in her heart she knew that Nicholas was right. Mixing with others was what she was short of. She would grant him that, but with regard to the therapy he'd suggested. . .he was way off course.

'Yes, I'd like that,' she told Cassandra. 'Are we going straight from here or going home to change?'

'We shan't bother changing,' the blonde sister-in-charge said. 'It's just a case of going for some pub grub to save us all cooking for once.

'Mike and his possessive fiancée were going to join us, but I'm afraid that Janice sees every other woman as competition—whether they're married or single,' she said with a wry smile. 'Which can't be very nice for him.'

As Rachel nodded her agreement she was wondering what his intended thought about Felice being under his nose all the time he was at the surgery, and on the heels of that thought came another. Janice just might have something to be concerned about there—on his part, anyway.

It was crowded in The Goose but the party from Springfield had booked a table and it wasn't difficult to find room for an extra one.

As her companions discussed the result of the cricket match, which had been won by the hospital team—to their gratification—Rachel looked around her. There was no sign of Nicholas and she was thankful that he hadn't had the same idea as the Springfield crowd. To have to face him so soon after their long, passionate embrace was more than she could face. In fact, if she never saw him again that would be fine.

It wouldn't, though, would it? If she was honest, she must admit that even though he was managing and overpowering he was different to any man she'd ever known, and he must be interested in her to some extent if he cared about her health and her appearance.

With regard to her state of mind, she wasn't too sure how concerned he was about *that*. It certainly hadn't been his top priority when he'd turned her into a quivering jelly earlier in the afternoon. Some therapy it had proved to be, and he must be crazy if he thought she'd believed him.

At that moment the door opened and he walked in, still in his cricketing whites. His face was bronzed from the afternoon sun and his blue gaze as vigilant as ever. As it raked the room it found her, sitting white-faced in the corner.

It had been a mistake to come here, to the focal point of the village, she thought raggedly. She might have known that he would appear. Why hadn't she gone straight home, as she'd intended?

To her relief, he made no attempt to join them. He merely nodded briefly, then turned to the bar. After downing a glass of lager thirstily, he left without looking in her direction again.

Gabriella Lassiter had been observing her with amused dark eyes, and when they got a moment together she said teasingly, 'Was Nick Page looking for you, Rachel?'

'No,' she said too quickly. 'I hardly know the man.'

The other girl smiled. 'Obviously my mistake, but I could have sworn. . .'

She broke off in mid-sentence. There was a commotion near the door and a man's voice shouted hoarsely, 'There's a fire at the hospital!'

The group at her table got to their feet in one movement, Rachel with them, and then they were running for their cars as the fire engine went whizzing past.

It seemed a lifetime before the neat, single-storey building came into view. She'd been dreading that an inferno would be awaiting them, but thick black smoke was coming from just the one area.

That, in itself, was a relief of sorts. If the fire brigade could control it—stop it from spreading before the flames and smoke reached other parts—the damage to life and property might be curtailed.

As Rachel flung herself out of the car she saw traumatised patients in their dressing-gowns crouched on the low stone wall of the hospital forecourt, while those confined to bed had been wheeled outside by the frantic weekend staff who were scurrying to and fro amongst them.

'Is everybody out?' Ethan Lassiter shouted as he ran towards them.

One of the sisters turned a petrified face to his. 'Everybody, except old Tommy Dyson. He'd gone to

the toilet and while he was there a fire started in the
small side-ward next to Geriatrics.'

'How, for God's sake?' he bellowed.

She looked away. 'A visitor had lit a cigarette for
the elderly patient in the side-ward just as they were
leaving, and he'd dozed off with it in his hand. It fell
onto the newspaper he'd been reading and set the bed
and the curtains around it alight.'

'Aagh! I don't believe it!' he groaned. 'Can't people
read? There are notices everywhere, forbidding smoking
and warning about the dangers of fire.'

'The man who caused the blaze has second-degree
burns—they're taking him to a burns unit in
Birmingham. Four of the patients from the main geriatric ward are in Casualty now, being treated for smoke
inhalation,' she explained chokily. 'The rest we managed to get out safely, but it was touch and go.'

Rachel and Cassandra joined him at that moment and
the horror of what was being said wiped the colour
from their faces.

Firemen were running to and fro, attaching their
hoses to the hydrants, and Ethan said desperately,
'Heads will roll for this! Do the fire brigade know that
Tommy's in there?'

'Yes. They know about them both,' the nurse replied.

'Both?' the two women chorused. 'Who else is
in there?'

'One of the consultants had stopped by to check on
a patient, and he was here when it started. He helped
with the evacuation, and when we realised that old
Tommy was still in there he went in to get him.'

Rachel felt a cold hand squeeze her heart. 'Who was
it?' she whispered, with dread making her legs go weak.

'It was Nicholas Page, and he's still in there.'

Her blood froze. It was only a short time since she'd

wished that she might never see him again, and now her wish might be granted.

I care about him, she thought frantically, and I'm going to lose him. The possibility that he might not feel the same didn't matter in that second. All that counted was that she should be given the chance to tell him that the cold, miserable exterior she'd been presenting wasn't really her. That she could be as warm and passionate as the next woman with a man who truly loved her.

As she looked around her she saw that Ethan and Cassandra had gone and only the smoke-grimed sister, a couple of junior nurses and the patients huddled in their blankets remained. Rachel realised that she'd been rooted to the spot in her despair when she should have been in there—looking for him, trying to save him—instead of bleating on about her own needs.

'Rachel!' his voice said suddenly from behind. 'What's wrong?'

He'd asked her that once before today, but in very different circumstances. Then he had been questioning her anger at his tongue-in-cheek efforts to rouse her out of her lethargy.

Now he was bringing her back from the brink of heartbreak and as she flung herself round to face him, taking in his singed hair and the smoke-blackened face with its red-rimmed eyes, hysterical relief made her say the first thing that came into her head.

'I might have known that you wouldn't let a small thing like a blazing inferno get the better of you,' she choked, fighting back the tears.

He tutted irritably. 'Thanks for the warm welcome! Though I'm warm enough already, after heaving the old man through the skylight and onto the roof with the fire licking at my heels.'

'How did you get out?' she croaked.

'The fire fighters brought us down on the far side of the building.'

'And Tommy?' she breathed.

'Grumbling that he'd never smelt anything that bad since he used to smoke Woodbines.'

'You need to be checked over,' she said quickly as she gathered her wits. 'Have you any burns or cuts?'

'I'll get one of the nurses to look me over,' he said abruptly, as if he'd done his bit by letting her see that he was all right and wasn't too chuffed at the reception he'd received.

'*I'll* do that,' she offered on a more decisive note. 'We'll go to the surgery. Or maybe Casualty at the Infirmary would be a better idea. There's no point in trying to sort you out here. The place is in chaos.'

'Yes, ma'am,' he said with deceptive meekness, 'and the surgery will do fine. I'm merely suffering from smoke inhalation, which took place when I went back into the building to look for Tommy. Once I'd found him and we moved upwards instead of out we were away from most of it.'

He smiled, his teeth flashing whitely in his blackened face. 'What do I look like, eh?'

'Your whites are no longer white, for one thing. I take it that you called in at Springfield on your way home from the cricket match,' she said as the shock-waves began to recede. 'As for the rest of you...you look like a leftover from the Black and White Minstrels.'

'Yeah? Well, don't be expecting me to go down on one knee singing *Mammy*. It's not my style.'

As she opened the car door for him she said, 'No, it's not, is it? Your style is taking charge, even if it means risking your life...or taking the local frump in hand.'

'And who might that be?' he asked chattily as he

eased himself into the passenger seat. 'You're surely not referring to yourself?'

'You know I am. So don't beat about the bush!'

'I would describe you as more of a crushed flower than a frump.'

'Really?'

'Yes, and we both know that if a flower is hardy enough it will bloom again.'

'And if it doesn't?'

'It becomes a scattering of useless petals.'

She didn't believe that they were having this conversation, but she'd started it, hadn't she? Nicholas wasn't to blame, and as she looked across at him Rachel saw that the palm of one of his hands was raw and blistered.

Alarm filled her. What other injuries had he received that he was making light of? If his hands were hurt he wouldn't be able to operate, and she could imagine how he would feel about that.

He was watching her expression. 'Stop worrying,' he said calmly. 'My hand got burnt because I had it up, protecting my face. I'll live to see another day.'

'It must be agonising,' she said contritely, 'and I've been babbling on about everything and nothing.'

She had gone past the turning for the surgery and he said, 'Hey, what's going on?'

'We're going to the Infirmary without delay. They have much better facilities than a local surgery can offer.' As he opened his mouth to protest, she added, 'Don't argue, Nicholas.'

It was the first time since they'd met that she'd felt in charge and—even though it was under distressing circumstances—it was a pleasant feeling to know that he was having to take *her* advice for once.

His voice broke into her deliberations. 'My friends call me Nick.'

'And?'

'I think we got past the stage of being just mere acquaintances earlier in the afternoon. Or have you forgotten?'

Forgotten? Was he joking? Yes. . .he probably was.

'No, I haven't forgotten,' she told him calmly. 'Although I'd have said it was more an exercise in lust than friendship.'

The red-rimmed eyes were unreadable in his grimy face, but his voice was casual enough as he said, 'Maybe you're right. I certainly never do anything without a reason, but for once my motives weren't as clear as they usually are.'

The amount of blistering on Nicholas's hand indicated first-degree burns. When the staff on the unit had satisfied themselves that there were no other areas needing treatment, an antibacterial dressing was placed over the affected area and his blood pressure and pulse rate checked.

While it was being done Rachel stood quietly to one side, expecting that at any moment he would take over—but he didn't. He submitted to the ministrations of the duty doctor and nursing staff with a restrained sort of impatience.

And he merely nodded, as if he'd already worked it out for himself, when the young registrar said, 'Fortunately, the degree of burns you have suffered isn't enough for there to be any great degree of fluid loss. If there had been we would have had to administer intravenous replacement.

'Any breathing problems?' he asked when the dressing had been applied.

'No,' Nicholas told him. 'I grabbed a blanket and held it over my nose and mouth, and I was only in the smoke for a matter of minutes.'

'But long enough to save the life of some old guy,
I'm told.'

He shrugged. 'Somebody had to go in after him and
the nurses had their hands full, bringing the rest of the
patients to safety.'

He got to his feet and looked around him at the burns
team. 'Thanks for your help, everyone,' he told them
and added, with an ironic smile, 'I won't say that I hope
I can do the same for you some time.'

When they got outside Mike's car was pulling up on
the Infirmary forecourt, and Rachel was surprised to
see Felice seated beside him.

'I went to the hall to tell them what had happened,'
he said as she ran towards her brother, 'and offered
to bring Felice here, as I guessed that this is where
you'd be.'

'What about Janice?' she asked. 'Where is she?'

'At home—feeling not too pleased that I've deserted
her, I'm afraid. When Cassie phoned to tell me what
had happened and what Nick had been involved in I
felt that I must go to Felice.' He glanced across at the
tall figure of Nicholas. 'Is he all right?'

'Yes, up to a point. Although his hand is quite badly
burnt. I would think that he won't be operating for a
couple of weeks. How about Springfield? What's the
damage?'

'Geriatric ward's in a bad state,' he said grimly. 'The
rest of the building is grimy but untouched by the fire.
Ethan and his staff have my sympathy.'

'They'll have to spread the patients around the other
hospitals until it's habitable again,' Nicholas said as he
joined them, with Felice eyeing him anxiously, 'but if
I know the management at Springfield it won't be for
long. Ethan Lassiter and his second-in-command won't
let the grass grow under their feet.'

'It sounds as if you didn't either,' Mike said

admiringly. 'Getting the old man out safely, without any great harm coming to him.'

'If I'd had time to think about it I might have wavered,' Nicholas said unconvincingly. 'It was a reflex action.' His eyes went to Rachel, and the message in them was for her alone. 'Come to think of it, that was the second thing I've done today that was entirely on impulse.'

# CHAPTER FIVE

'I'LL take Felice to Springfield to pick up your car, if you like,' Mike offered as Nicholas settled himself into Rachel's vehicle once more.

Nicholas had been into his rooms at the Infirmary to wash while they'd been there and was no longer so grimy, but his clothes, the singed hair and the dressing on his hand were grim reminders of what had taken place earlier. Yet he was sitting beside her, as if they'd just been for an evening run.

Tenderness unwound inside her. Twice in one afternoon he'd put his job before his own concerns—in the first instance going to the hospital to check on a patient, and in the second his cool rescue of old Tommy.

'Thanks, Mike. I'd appreciate it, if you would,' he replied. 'It will save me the hassle of having to get it collected tomorrow.'

As she drove back to Larksby Hall in the mellow summer evening he was silent and she eyed him anxiously. Was he beginning to feel the effects of the smoke and his burnt hand? she wondered, but when at last he did speak it was clear that his mind was running on its usual fast track.

'You haven't asked me who I'd gone to visit at Springfield,' he said briefly. 'Or have you guessed?'

'Rita?' she questioned.

'Yes, it was Rita, and I have good news for you. The numbness is receding. Whether she will regain full use of her legs is not yet clear but, with physiotherapy and a corset to support the damaged vertebrae once we get her mobile again, there could be a good chance of recovery.'

'How did the staff manage to get her out?' Rachel asked, ashamed that her concern for the man beside her had blotted out every other consideration.

'In Rita's case, they wheeled the bed out. You wouldn't have seen her, as she was at the other side of the hospital to where I found you in a trance-like state...and I'd still like to know what was wrong.'

'I'm amazed that you need to ask!' she exclaimed. 'I was trying to cope with the news that you were somewhere inside the blazing geriatric ward!'

'And debating whether you'd be glad or sorry if you never saw me again?'

Her face flamed. He was dangerously near the truth, but not in that way—never that!

Nicholas was watching her expression. 'So I'm right. You wouldn't have been sorry if I'd been removed from the scene?'

Rachel pulled in by the roadside and turned to face him. 'That remark was in extremely bad taste,' she said quietly. 'I would have been devastated if anything had happened to you, just as I would have been if anyone else had come to harm in the fire.'

'Which puts me well and truly in my place,' he said with a dry smile. 'I'm never going to get too big for my boots with you around, am I?'

'I wouldn't imagine that anything *I* might say or do would influence you,' she flashed back, aware that they were becoming involved in personalities again. 'You're a law unto yourself.'

His face became still. 'So that's what you think. That I believe everyone is out of step, except me?'

She didn't answer. If she said yes he might take offence and the frail rapport between them would be broken, and if she said no, he would take it that she'd joined the Nicholas Page fan club.

But she had, hadn't she? He was gradually breaking down her defences, and if he were to touch her now she would melt again like she had during the afternoon in the clearing beneath the trees.

By the time they got back to the hall the sun was an orange blue on the horizon and lights were on in some of the downstairs rooms.

'Can I offer you a coffee or maybe something stronger?' he asked as she pulled up in front of his imposing residence, and he unrolled the long length of him from the passenger seat.

'No, thanks just the same,' she said quickly. 'I'm sure that you must be more than ready to relax after what happened earlier.'

'Yes, I am,' he said decisively. 'More than ready, but you could have a chat with Meg while I'm making myself presentable and Felice will be back soon.'

Rachel could feel herself weakening, but she stuck to her guns. 'No, really, Nicholas. I don't want to intrude. I'm just thankful that you're all right, apart from that.' Her eyes went to his bandaged hand.

'Suit yourself,' he said evenly. 'And, as you won't come inside, I'll say it now.'

'What?' she asked warily.

'Thanks for taking me to the Infirmary.'

She felt a lump come up in her throat. He didn't have to voice his thanks. It had been the least she could do. The memory of the anguished moments when he'd been inside the burning building surfaced again, and with it the admission that she'd made to herself then.

She *did* care for him. She cared a lot. . .and she didn't want to. Falling in love with someone as high-powered as Nicholas Page wasn't going to do anything for her bruised heart or her peace of mind. But it was happening, as irrevocably as night followed day, and she didn't know what she was going to do about it.

'I've been only too happy to be of service,' she told him gravely and, with the feeling that she'd been rather churlish in the way she'd refused his invitation, she went on, 'I'd be delighted to see the inside of the hall some other time when you are less fraught.'

Dark brows rose at that. 'I am not fraught, as you describe it, Dr Rachel Maddox,' he said irritably. 'And will you please stop treating me like one of your patients.'

'All right,' she retorted, 'but, if you want me to do that, please do me a favour. If you won't let *me* look after you—look after yourself. After all, I would imagine that in your opinion no one can do it better.'

He laughed low in his throat, but didn't take her up on the comment. Instead, surveying the hall with a critical eye, he told her, 'I'll show you round this place any time you like. It's impressive, but far too big for the three of us and Toby.

'I bought it at a knock-down price, but hadn't really thought of living in it myself. Yet, somehow or other, when I moved to this area from up north I never got around to looking for anything smaller and we deposited ourselves here temporarily. As you can see, that still applies but I feel that the place could be put to much better use than as at present.'

'Such as?' she asked, aware that she was delaying his cleaning-up process. 'A private patients' clinic, maybe?'

'I don't see people privately. It's against my principles,' he said laconically.

'I'm not with you,' she said in surprise.

'I only work through the NHS. That way, everyone gets a fair deal when it comes to my services.'

This man was full of surprises, she thought, and would, no doubt, continue to be so. He was high-handed, decisive and on top of his job but not prepared to make full his coffers at the expense of the suffering public, and she couldn't help but admire and respect those sort of principles.

'So, what will you do with the hall when you find something smaller?' she asked, bringing her mind back to the matter on hand.

'I haven't decided. Felice has suggested a refuge for battered wives, or a home for unmarried mothers.'

Rachel goggled at him. '*She* made those suggestions?'

He gave a wry smile. 'Yes. There are times when she's quite human.'

'I think that both ideas are excellent, and she should be congratulated for her foresight,' Rachel told him, accepting that his sister was just as unpredictable as he.

'Yes, well, being an unmarried mother herself, I suppose she has realised that it's not a bed of roses—and my sister's circumstances are a great deal better than most.'

She couldn't argue with that. Felice *was* fortunate to have no apparent money worries and the support of Meg and Nicholas.

'My not having private patients hasn't made me too popular with one or two of the other consultants,' he went on to say, 'but. . .'

'You're not going to lose any sleep about that,' she finished off for him.

He flexed his shoulders and, running his hands through his singed hair, said, 'Correct. You read my mind once again, Rachel Maddox.'

'That will be the day!' she exclaimed laughingly.

'You think so?'

'Yes, I do.'

'Right. Well, in that case, as I can't entice you into

my lair, I'm going to depart because I'm desperate to get under the shower.'

Rachel nodded. 'Goodnight, Nicholas,' she said softly. Turning the car round, she drove it back along the winding drive to where the mullioned windows of the lodge shone gold in the sun's last rays.

Mike called round on Sunday morning and when she expressed surprise at seeing him he said, 'I've just been up to the hall to see young Toby. Felice called me out as he was covered in a rash, but I was able to assure her that the cause was nothing more sinister than his teeth.'

Rachel eyed him thoughtfully. They weren't on call at weekends. There was an emergency service available, but it looked as if Nicholas's unpredictable sister had phoned her partner at home and he had come out personally to visit the baby.

He seemed in no hurry to depart, so she made coffee for them and took it out into the garden. As they sat in silence amongst the sweet smell of summer flowers, with blue tits providing their own splash of colour in an old apple tree, Rachel was aware that Mike wasn't his usual serene self, and she had a feeling that she knew why.

'I've made a big mistake, Rachel,' he said at last, 'and, although I've only known you for a short time, I feel that you're the only person I have the courage to tell.'

She nodded gravely but didn't speak, and he went on, 'I'll bet you can guess what I'm going to say.' When she still didn't have any comment to make, he continued, 'It's Janice. I don't love her. I let myself become involved with her on the rebound, so to speak.

'I'd been in love with Cassandra Marsland for some time, or thought I was, and when she married Bevan I felt really miserable—as if no woman was ever going to fancy me. It was then that Janice made a play for me and, like a fool, I let her, knowing full well that a marriage is no good without real affection.' He sighed. 'And now I want out, and yet can't bear the thought of hurting the girl.'

'You'll be hurting Janice far more if you marry her against your will,' Rachel said carefully. 'If I were you, I would wait for the right moment and then tell her. You're a kind man, Mike. When the time comes you'll know how to cause her as little distress as possible but, whatever you do, don't let wedding plans go any further. That would be most unfair.'

He nodded miserably. 'Yes, you're right. I must tell her as soon as the opportunity presents itself.'

'There isn't any other reason why you want to break off your engagement, is there?' she asked gently.

The colour rose on his fair skin. 'No, of course not,' he said firmly, but the look in his eyes didn't match the definite tone.

When he'd gone Rachel sat gazing into space, her mind going over their conversation, and there was relief in her that Mike had realised that marriage to the tight-lipped Janice wasn't what he wanted. But as the vision of another woman with a petulant, dark attractiveness came to mind she had a feeling that her partner might just be contemplating jumping out of the frying pan into the fire.

In the middle of the afternoon Rachel walked up to the hall. It was something she wouldn't have done in normal circumstances, as she was determined to keep her involvement with Nicholas to a minimum. Otherwise, Mike wouldn't be the only one who was contemplating changing one distressing relationship for another. But she wanted to make sure that Nicholas was no worse after the fire at Springfield.

She had spoken to Gabriella Lassiter briefly first thing and had been told that Ethan was at an emergency meeting of the Area Health Authority, where plans were being discussed with regard to getting the hospital back to its normal working conditions as speedily as possible.

'How is he taking it?' Rachel had asked.

'He's devastated,' Gabriella said soberly. 'He can't believe that a patient was left alone long enough to set the place on fire. But there is always the human element, and the nurses were busy dealing with an epileptic fit and a suspected heart attack simultaneously when the blaze started.'

As the hall came into view, Rachel stopped to admire it. It was a beautiful building of golden stone with arched windows and a high roof, and in a moment of envy she thought how marvellous it must be to live in such a beautiful house.

Yet Nicholas hadn't seemed too enraptured with it. He'd spoken as if it was merely a place to live and too big for them, at that. But, of course, home is where the heart is, she thought soberly, remembering how empty her own house had seemed when there'd been no love in it any more. Maybe Nick's heart wasn't home either.

As she stood deep in thought beneath the shade of a huge willow tree Rachel heard voices, and round a bend in the drive came a man and woman with arms entwined. Her heart jolted. Her mind had been full of him, and now Nicholas was here—and on very familiar terms with his companion, from the looks of it.

Here was the magnetic force again, she thought as his gaze met hers, taking in her trim, fine-boned figure in close-fitting jeans and a cotton top.

'Hello there, Dr Maddox,' he said crisply.

Rachel's eyes widened. He'd been quick enough to use her first name on only short acquaintance but now, because he had a willowy blonde on his arm, she was relegated to the ranks once more.

'Hello, Nick,' she said with perverse familiarity.

He indicated his companion. 'This is Gaynor Kingsley, a very good friend of mine.' To the fair woman he said, 'Rachel Maddox, one of our local general practitioners.'

As the two women shook hands Rachel was taking stock of the newcomer, and liking what she saw. The woman wasn't a raving beauty but she had a nice smile and a smooth, serene face, and she envied her. Not because of her physical attributes, but because she appeared to be on very good terms with Nicholas.

'I was on my way to see you,' she told him with a crispness to match his own. 'To enquire how you are after yesterday's episode.'

Nicholas looked down at his injured hand. 'It's a bit painful,' he admitted, 'but nothing that is going to bother me unduly, I hope. I won't be operating until it's healed, of course, and on the strength of that I'm going to stay with Gaynor and her folks for a few days. One of my assistants can deal with my case load.'

'That will be nice,' she said with false heartiness. 'And where might that be?'

'Jersey. My family have an hotel there,' Gaynor told her, as the winning smile flashed out again.

Depression was falling on Rachel like a heavy, grey blanket. So he was going away with this pleasant, golden woman, whom he'd known for a long time. This was the man who'd said that his friends had dropped away because he was never available, but this one hadn't.

What was it that Meg Jardine had said as they'd driven home from the fashion show? That, no matter how busy he was, Nick would make time for Gaynor Kingsley. . .now that she'd appeared on the scene again.

'Shall I change the dressing?' Rachel asked abruptly,

bringing her thoughts in line with more basic matters.

'No. Leave it,' he said casually. 'I'll deal with it, if I think it necessary. You're off duty. Enjoy what's left of your weekend.'

She eyed him bleakly. There wasn't much chance of that, with the thought of him swanning around Jersey with Gaynor and Mike in the depths of gloom over his tangled love life—not to mention her own feeling of rejection which was never far away. All that, in total, made her feel that it would take a mammoth effort to raise enthusiasm over anything.

'Yes, I'll try to do that,' she told him flatly. 'And now I'll be on my way but, first, how is Toby? Mike called on his way home and said that Felice had sent for him.'

'Yes, she did,' he said with a dry smile. 'Your worthy partner said that it's the baby's teeth again, but there's nothing to worry about as long as she keeps an eye on his temperature.

'She calmed down once he'd been. That sister of mine is all or nothing. She either goes all day and barely sees the child, or she's frantic about his well-being.'

'She's very young,' Rachel said, 'and when I spoke to Felice she told me that she had a difficult birth.'

'Yes, she did,' he agreed briefly. 'I don't need reminding of that. We almost lost her, and that is why Meg and I put up with her fluctuating moods. Fortunately, she's seemed much better since starting at the surgery so maybe being occupied is what she needed.'

'When are you going to Jersey?' she asked, her mind leaping ahead.

'This evening,' he informed her, and added, to her surprise, 'Don't worry about Rita. I've given my assistant her case notes and told him to keep you informed. She's still at Springfield. I checked this morning. Apparently, part of the hospital wasn't fire-damaged and she's in there, which pleases me greatly as I definitely don't want her moved until the vertebrae have settled down.'

So he hadn't been idle since she'd brought him home last night, Rachel thought. Nick had been arranging his clinics, checking on his patients and getting in touch with Gaynor—unless it was she who'd heard about his part in the fire and had come post-haste to check up on *him*.

If she had it made two of them, but her own role seemed to be of minor importance and she decided that the closeness she and Nick had shared the previous day, including the mad moments they'd spent in each other's arms at the cricket match, must have been a figment of her imagination.

'Enjoy your stay in Jersey, Nick,' she said quietly, and to his companion, 'Nice to have met you, Gaynor.'

Rachel felt as if his eyes were boring into her back as she walked away, but she put it down to imagination. When she glanced quickly over her shoulder as she reached the gate of the lodge the drive behind her was empty.

She went to Springfield the next day to check up on Rita, and found that the fire damage was much more evident than it had been during the blaze of Saturday afternoon. As she gazed through where the windows of the geriatric ward had been all she could see was charred woodwork and blackened walls.

The majority of the patients had been transferred elsewhere, but cases who required uninterrupted bed-rest—like the buxom receptionist—were situated in the day-ward which had escaped damage to any great degree. The administrative section of the hospital had also escaped the blaze, and as Rachel passed Ethan's office he called her name.

As she turned he was standing in the doorway, looking tired and grim, with Cassandra close behind him, and her heart went out to these two whose efficiency and hard work kept the small community hospital running on oiled wheels.

They had been let down by circumstances—the stupidity of visitors giving a lighted cigarette to a sick, disorientated old man, two emergencies occurring at the same moment to occupy the staff and the fact that it had been the weekend when the fire occurred and neither of them had been there to take over and maybe exercise a speedier control of the situation.

Cassandra looked the worse of the two. She was very pale, with dark circles under her eyes, and literally drooping with tiredness.

'You need to get some rest, Cassandra,' Rachel told her firmly. 'You look all in.'

The blonde senior sister brushed a lock of stray hair off her brow and smiled wearily. 'I'm all right.'

Ethan was eyeing her worriedly. 'You're not, Cassie. I've been so bogged down with all this that I haven't been fair to you. Do what Rachel says. Go home. We've been here all weekend until God knows what hour, and if you end up being ill we'll have achieved nothing.'

He went on, 'We might feel as if we're in the middle of a nightmare here at Springfield but there has been no loss of life, and that's the main thing. Bricks and mortar can soon be replaced, but people can't. So do go home. Bevan and Mark need you just as much as Springfield does.'

They were both awaiting her reply, but it seemed that Cassandra had nothing to say. With a gentle sighing sort of noise, she slid down on to the carpet and lay at their feet.

In the same second Bevan came striding into the room, and when he saw his wife he was across the carpet in a flash. 'What's happened?' he cried as they bent over her unconscious form.

'She's fainted,' Rachel said. 'We were trying to persuade her to go home when she suddenly collapsed.'

'It's my fault,' Ethan said contritely. 'I should have realised she was on the verge of collapse, but Cassie always seems so strong.'

'She is, usually,' Bevan said raggedly as his wife began to open her eyes, 'but there's something that you're not aware of. . . Cassandra is pregnant.'

Ethan's distress increased. 'Oh! My God! Why didn't she tell me? How far on is she?'

'Four months,' Bevan told him as he took her limp hand in his, 'and she didn't tell you because she didn't want to let you down at a time like this.' He groaned. 'I fell in with her wishes, against my better judgement, and between us she and I could have jeopardised the child that we long for.'

Cassandra had heard what he said and she lifted her hand and touched his lips gently. 'Don't worry, darling. It will be all right. I'm just tired. It's not as if I'm bleeding or anything sinister like that.' To Ethan, whose face was a mask of horror, she said, 'Don't blame yourself, Ethan. I *will* go home and rest, as you advise, and I'll be right as rain in the morning. Why don't you go home to Gabriella for a few hours? There isn't a lot you can do for the moment.'

'No, I suppose not,' he muttered. He turned to Rachel. 'There is to be another meeting tomorrow of the authority chiefs and the estates department, regarding the fire damage. It has been convened with all haste, and I'm hoping that the necessary repairs and refurbishment will be done with as much speed. As Cassie says, until then there isn't a lot we can do, except to see to it that what's left of the hospital is functioning as well as can be expected.'

'What a carry-on, eh, Dr Maddox?' Rita said when Rachel espied her bed in a corner of the crowded day-ward. 'Nicholas Page had come to Springfield to see me, and he ends up strolling into the blaze like Superman to rescue some old fellow!'

Rachel hid a smile. Rita's sense of drama was obviously well developed. 'Yes, what about it? It was a very courageous thing to do. But what about you, Rita? Any more movement?'

The receptionist smiled. 'Yes, thank God! I can feel my legs again. The physiotherapist says it will be some weeks before I can break into a gallop—and they're going to measure me for a steel corset—but I'm getting there, and that's all that matters.

'I believe you've got our hero's sister doing my job?' she said anxiously. 'I want to come back when I'm better, you know, Doctor.'

'And you will,' Rachel told her soothingly. 'Felice Page is only filling in while you're away.'

Rita's face cleared. 'Thank goodness for that. I love working at the surgery, and we need my wages to help the family budget.'

As Rachel drove back to the practice she wondered if Rita realised just how lucky she'd been. A more serious injury could have resulted in the spinal cord being severed by the damaged vertebrae—or by a blood clot, or even by accumulated fluid—but in her case the X-rays had shown that there was no likelihood of anything moving, and she should eventually make a complete recovery.

It seemed strange to see long legs in sheer tights under the desk behind Reception when she got back, instead of Rita's sensible twenty denier, and when Felice looked up Rachel said the first thing that came into her head.

'You'll be quiet up at the hall with Nicholas away in Jersey,' she commented.

'Yes, we are,' Felice agreed. 'He said to invite some people round for company, but I can't be bothered. Everything is too much of an effort since I had Toby.'

'Yet you took on the job here?' Rachel questioned. '*And* are doing it very well.'

Felice gave a buttoned-up sort of smile. 'I *was* a secretary when I was in Geneva, you know, *not* the tea girl, but all that changed when I discovered I was pregnant. Toby's father wanted me to have an abortion. He said he was too old to start with a family again, but the truth of it was that he didn't want to leave his wife. . .and so, just to be awkward, I carried on with the pregnancy.'

'That seems a strange reason for bringing a new life into the world,' Rachel said. 'What did your brother have to say about it?'

Blue eyes that were so like his met her own. 'Quite a lot. He was furious. Nick can't bear the waste of human life, but neither did he approve of my reasoning.'

'And what do you see for yourself in the future?' she asked curiously.

Felice smiled and Rachel thought how it changed the sulky lines of her face. 'Not so long ago I didn't see anything to get excited about, but now my vision is clearing.'

'Really?'

'Yes, I've discovered that all men aren't rats. There's Nick, for instance, who puts up with my whims and tantrums for Toby's sake. . .and someone else, too, who doesn't treat me as just a body, for the use of.'

'I see,' Rachel said slowly, with a very good idea who that person was, and her misgivings about his love life returned. 'But surely the main person in *your* life is your son?'

Felice's face clouded. 'Sometimes it is, and some-times it isn't. I never knew what real pain was until I had Toby, and if Nick hadn't been with me I'd have given up and died.'

Serious though the discussion was, Rachel had to conceal a smile again. Here was another dramatist. Their two receptionists would make a good pair in that respect, though they were the exact opposite in every other way, she thought as a vision of Rita's plump thighs came to mind.

'Meg said that Gaynor is a very old friend of your brother's?' she said casually, ashamed that she was doing the very thing she abhorred by gossiping about him, and yet unable to help herself.

Her heart leapt as Felice said with equal nonchalance, 'Yes, she's been around for some time, but if Nick had wanted her he'd have done something about it by now.' But Rachel's spirits took a dive as she went on to say, 'Although, having said that, she's only recently become available again after having gone through a messy divorce.'

'He doesn't like anything messy,' Rachel said without thinking, and was rewarded with a surprised stare.

'I don't know how you come to be aware of that,' Felice said, 'but, yes, you're right. He likes everything to be organised and orderly. That's why *I* drive him insane.'

As she went into her consulting-room to start after-noon surgery Rachel thought that being involved with two messy divorcees was hardly Nicholas's style but, then, he wasn't involved with her, was he? It was on the cards that he'd seen her merely as 'a body, for the use of', to quote Felice, that day at the cricket match. . .

As an anxious mother with a feverish small girl appeared in answer to her buzzer she put him firmly out of her mind.

# CHAPTER SIX

THE few days that Nicholas had promised himself in Jersey became a fortnight and, during that time, Rachel carried out her duties in the practice with her usual cool competence, even though she was aware of a nagging feeling of incompleteness inside her.

It seemed strange not to be bumping into him at every turn, as had previously been the case, and she broke through the protective barrier of her reserve to ask Felice how he was enjoying the break.

On the first occasion his sister lifted her head from the practice appointments book and told her, 'He seems to be having a whale of a time with all that sun, sea, and. . .'

'Sex?' Rachel prompted casually.

Felice laughed. 'I was going to say "seduction", but I don't think that would apply to Nick. He's always been able to attract women, like bees to a honey-pot.'

'And so why has he never married?' Rachel asked tartly, angry to have left herself wide open for whatever degree of disenchantment Felice sent her way.

'Big brother is very choosy, for one thing,' she was informed, 'and, for another, his job always seems to get in the way. The glamorous chicks who've pursued him in the past have all been on the lookout for nine-to-fivers, with weekends at home, and you—as much as anyone—will understand that those are not his working hours.'

Mike appeared at that moment, and Rachel was aware that Felice's attention had switched to her partner. Had he broken the glad tidings to Janice yet? she wondered.

If he hadn't then it was high time that he did. She wasn't keen on the girl, but she could sympathise with her. There was no lonelier feeling on earth than to be rejected by the person one cared for.

When she questioned him about it later Mike admitted gloomily that he'd done the deed the previous evening and, after witnessing the tantrum that his fiancée had thrown and wrestling with his guilt, he'd had a very disturbed night—a fact which was manifesting itself in his shadowed eyes and bristle-covered chin.

'At least you've done it,' Rachel consoled. 'Things can only get better now, and don't start on a guilt trip, Mike. I wouldn't have said it before, but I will now. You deserve someone much, much nicer than Janice, and when you find the right one you'll know. It won't be like the crush you had for Cassandra or the lukewarm romance with Janice. It will knock you for six!'

He gave a tired grin. 'You sound as if you have first-hand experience. Was that how you felt when you met your husband?'

She nodded, aware that she'd fallen into a pitfall of her own making. There *had* been a spontaneous attraction between Rob and herself when they'd first met, but they'd been young and immature in those days. Although *she* had grown up in the busy world that called for her skills *he* hadn't and, because they hadn't been keeping pace with each other, the marriage had ground to a halt.

But it hadn't been Rob to whom she'd been referring. Another man had been in her mind. In fact, these days he was rarely out of it. He was the one who'd knocked *her* for six—brought a shaft of light into her desolation—and, with a surge of weary frustration, she wished him home again. . .alone. . .and fancy-free.

Any surmises as to what Nicholas might be doing in

Jersey only surfaced in the evenings when she had a precious couple of hours to herself, and then it was a case of deciding one minute that whatever he was doing it didn't concern her and in the next admitting that it did. . .and she wished that it didn't.

At this particular time a rare outbreak of bacterial meningitis in the nearby town was causing concern amongst the population, and Rachel and Mike were on the lookout for young patients with severe headache, fever and nausea or vomiting. But so far the village had kept clear of the deadly infection, even though most of the teenagers attended the large comprehensive school in the centre of the town.

That was until a humid summer morning when Rachel was called out to a small cottage on the outskirts of the village. Surgery had been mostly familiar ailments—among them a painful in-growing toenail which was going to require minor surgery, a couple of hay fever sufferers and a case of over-exposure to the sun— and it was just as the last patient was leaving that Felice put the call through.

A worried man's voice at the other end informed her that his eight-year-old son was ill, and when he described the symptoms her heart sank.

'I'll come immediately,' she said. 'Has the receptionist taken your name and address?'

On being assured that she had, Rachel collected her bag and—after a quick word with Mike—proceeded to the home of the sick child.

She was hoping that she was wrong. That it might be a twenty-four hour virus or something similar, but the moment she saw the boy her hopes were dashed. He had all the classic symptoms of bacterial meningitis—a blotchy red rash, stiff neck, severe head pain and he was vomiting.

The father was hovering anxiously as she examined

the boy, and when she'd finished he said hoarsely, 'It's not this meningitis thing, is it, Doctor?'

Rachel eyed him levelly. 'At this moment I don't know, but it could be. However, I don't think we should jump to any conclusions until tests have been carried out on your son. Have you a telephone?'

The worried parent, a cowman employed on the Jarvis farm, pointed towards the kitchen. 'It's on the dresser.'

'I'm sending for an ambulance,' Rachel told him. 'The doctors at the Infirmary will do a lumbar puncture to remove a small amount of cerebrospinal fluid from the spinal chord, and that will tell them if it *is* meningitis.'

'And if it isn't?'

'It will be a cause for relief all round,' she told him with a sympathetic smile.

Joe Hamer turned away and blew his nose noisily. 'These are the times when we miss his mother,' he choked.

'Is she not here, then?' she asked carefully.

'Naw. She went off with some fancy-pants double-glazing salesman.'

'I see, and is there no one you can turn to for help?'

'There's Mrs Jarvis up at the farm. She used to be matron at the cottage hospital. She's bin real good to young Sam an' me.'

'Yes. I know the lady. Why don't I give her a ring, then?'

He shook his head. 'Naw. She's got a young 'un herself an' if what our Sam's got is catchin' hers might get it.

'I'll manage. My ma is away on holiday but she'll be home in a flash if she knows there's somethin' wrong with young Sam and, between the two of us, we'll cope.' As the boy moaned fretfully he looked down at his son's flushed face. 'Just as long as he gets better, eh, Doctor?'

She was spared having to offer the reassurance that the man was pleading for by the arrival of the ambulance, and as the sick child was stretchered into it Rachel prayed that quick treatment with intravenous antibiotics would save the boy's life if the test results showed meningitis.

Any further than that she wasn't prepared to think at this point. It was no use considering what else it might be until the lumbar puncture had been performed, but she was ninety-nine per cent sure that the cowman's son was suffering from meningococcal meningitis.

The report from the Infirmary confirmed Rachel's worst fears, and during the days that followed she and Mike made sure that all those who had been in close contact with their young patient were given antibiotics.

They discussed possible vaccination but because the strains of bacteria responsible for the disease were so many and varied they felt it wiser to treat immediate contacts, rather than take a stab in the dark with a vaccination programme—unless there were signs of an epidemic in the village.

When, by the end of the week, no further cases had been reported in the town—and the cowman's son was the only case from the village—the two doctors began to breathe more easily.

During this time Rachel was in contact with the anguished father. After calling at the cottage a couple of times and finding it deserted, she had eventually tracked him down at the Infirmary.

Bleary-eyed and unshaven, he was hunched on a bench in one of the waiting-rooms and—after confirming with the doctor in charge that the boy was beginning to show some signs of improvement—she'd persuaded him to go home for a short period.

'Have you managed to get in touch with your mother?' Rachel asked as she drove him back to the village.

'Yes,' he muttered. 'She's home. She's been at the hospital with me, but I sent her to get some rest as there was nothing she could do.'

'That was sensible,' Rachel told him, 'but you've got to think about yourself too, Joe. If you collapse under the strain there'll be only your mother to look after the boy when he comes out.'

His head had jerked up at that. 'So you think he's going to get better, Doctor?'

'He survived the first twenty-four hours, which are always critical, and the doctors—although not committing themselves—are pleased with his progress,' she told him guardedly. 'And so, yes, God willing, I do.'

At that the cowman had bent his head and wept, and Rachel had told him gently, 'Let it all out, Joe. You'll feel better afterwards.'

When they got back to his cottage his mother was there, anxiously waiting for news. Leaving him to her ministrations, Rachel had driven off—her relief at the improvement in the boy's condition almost as great as theirs.

Towards the end of Nicholas's second week away Rachel was aware of a procession of cars going past the lodge late one evening, and she deduced that his sister must have taken his advice and invited friends round.

Music drifting across the lawns and the murmur of voices gave credence to her assumption, and she wondered just what sort of an evening Felice had arranged.

One thing was for certain, Rachel thought with wry humour as she went upstairs to her solitary bed, it wouldn't be a hot-pot supper. It was more likely to be cocktails on the terrace, followed by shrimp vol-au-vents and strawberries and cream.

After a while the music became louder and the sub-dued voices changed to noisy laughter. Rachel hoped that the teething baby wouldn't be disturbed but, then, Meg would be there for him, wouldn't she? With a sigh, she climbed into bed and lay, wide-eyed, looking up at the ceiling.

Had Mike been invited to the social event on her doorstep? she wondered. He hadn't said anything but she vowed that she would ask him in the morning, if only to satisfy her curiosity.

He'd been subdued since breaking off his engage-ment to Janice and she knew that he felt guilty about it but, as she'd told him when first he'd confessed his doubts, it would have been much worse for the girl if he'd entered into a marriage that he didn't want.

On the brink of oblivion, she was brought back to wakefulness by someone hammering on her front door. As Rachel hurriedly slipped into a robe and went to investigate she found Felice on the doorstep, looking flushed and agitated.

'Can you come, Rachel?' she asked in a voice that was just the least bit slurred. 'Meg has fallen and I think her leg is broken.'

'Yes, of course,' she said immediately. 'Give me a couple of minutes to get some clothes on and I'll be right with you.'

As they went up the drive Rachel was aware that the music had stopped, and she wondered what had been going on inside the hall for Meg to have injured herself at this hour as it was well past midnight.

As if reading her thoughts, Felice explained uncom-fortably, 'She came downstairs to get a drink for Toby and one of the guys started waltzing her around the

room, but he'd had too much to drink and he fell over,
dragging her down with him.'

'That's disgusting,' Rachel said acidly. 'What an irresponsible thing to do to an elderly lady. You should
take better care of her!'

Felice averted her eyes, but from the toss of her head
it appeared to Rachel that she was more peeved at being
chastised than concerned about the accident.

'It wasn't *my* fault,' she said sulkily.

'It was if you can't control your guests,' Rachel persisted angrily. 'Obviously Mike isn't one of them, or
you wouldn't have come for me.'

'No, he isn't,' was the reply. 'I invited him but he
refused.'

'And you were disappointed?'

Her companion was really on the defensive now. 'No,
of course not!'

Meg was lying where she'd fallen on the carpet in a
lofty panelled hallway. She looked pale and in obvious
pain. When Rachel saw the position she was in she
decided that it was the hip, rather than the leg, which
had been fractured.

'Don't try to move, Meg,' she told her gently. 'I
think you may have a fractured femur. I'm going to
ring for an ambulance.'

A youth with a crop of blond curls was slumped
in a chair nearby and as Rachel straightened up, after
inspecting the leg, he mumbled, 'It was just a joke that
misfired.'

She eyed him coldly, wishing that Nicholas was at
home to take control. There would have been none of
this if he'd been around but he was still sampling the
delights of Jersey, as far as she knew. As for herself,
she could do without being involved in the kind of

fiasco which had resulted in an elderly lady being injured.

When the ambulance arrived Rachel spoke briefly with the paramedics and they lifted Meg carefully into the vehicle, with both legs strapped together to prevent any jolting of the injured hip.

'What about Toby if it turns out that I *have* fractured my hip?' the injured nanny asked anxiously as Felice hovered by her side.

The attractive single mother would have to mind her own child then, Rachel thought grimly, but she'd reckoned without Felice's determination to keep the job at the practice.

'I'll take him to work with me,' she said quickly with a defiant glance at Rachel. 'That is, if Rachel and Mike don't mind.'

Deciding that she'd had quite enough of Nicholas's sister for one night and not wanting to upset Meg, Rachel said flatly, 'If Meg is going to be temporarily incapacitated you'll have to discuss the situation with Mike. He's the senior partner. I'll fall in with whatever he decides.' She had a gut feeling, though, that any decision *he* was asked to make would be acceptable to Felice.

'I'll come with you, Meg,' Felice said suddenly as they stood by the open doors of the ambulance and added, with a wary glance at Rachel, 'That is, if you'll stay with Toby until I get back. I'll tell the others that the party's over. In fact, it was over the moment Meg fell, especially for Dominic. He's really sorry.'

'And so he should be,' Rachel said unrelentingly and then went on in a milder tone, 'Yes, of course I'll stay with Toby but, really, *I* ought to go with Meg. I *am* one of the village GPs.'

Felice shook her head stubbornly and, faced with the

girl's determination to accompany Meg to the infirmary, Rachel gave in.

When the subdued guests had left silence settled on the house, and Rachel went quietly upstairs to check on Toby. According to Felice, Meg had come downstairs to get him a drink so obviously he must have been awake, but when she gazed down into the cot he was asleep again—tiny fists bunched and long lashes smudged against his cheeks.

She sighed. Her arms had gone out to him instinctively as the longing to hold the soft sweetness of him against her took over, but she could hardly awaken the little one from sleep to satisfy her maternal cravings.

It seemed strange to be here alone in the house that belonged to Nicholas. He'd invited her in here once and she'd refused because earlier he'd been involved in the fire at Springfield. Although that fact had seemed to bother her more than it had him.

As she walked along a spacious landing towards the top of a wide curving staircase she saw that the door of what she guessed to be the master bedroom was firmly shut, and for an insane moment she craved to go inside—to look around the room where he slept and kept his personal belongings, and which would undoubtedly have his own particular stamp on it.

But there was no way that she would invade his privacy in such a manner, especially in his absence, and so she went downstairs and sat in a comfortable chair—in a sitting-room which was as big as the whole of the lodge put together—to wait until there was news from Felice.

She rang at half past one, with the information that Rachel's diagnosis had been correct. 'Meg *has* got a fractured femur,' she said stiltedly. 'She's just been X-rayed, and it shows that the bone ends at the neck of the femur are displaced. A Dr Beckman will operate tomorrow to realign them, and a metal plate will be inserted.'

Rachel nodded in the empty room. 'Good. It sounds as if they have it all organised, so you'll be back as soon as Meg is settled into one of the wards?' she questioned.

'Yes. Another hour or so should see me back at the hall.' There was silence for a moment and then Felice asked, 'Is Toby all right?'

'Fine,' Rachel told her evenly. 'I've just checked on him.'

'Nick will be furious when he knows what's happened,' Felice said morosely, 'although he *did* tell me to invite some of the golf club crowd round if I got bored.'

'And that was what you did,' Rachel said drily. 'It's a pity that Mike didn't accept your invitation. He would have been on hand when Meg fell. Although, having said that, if he had been at your party he wouldn't have allowed such a thing to happen.'

'I'm really to blame, aren't I?' the voice at the other end of the line said glumly. 'I can't do anything right. I only arranged the party as an excuse to invite Mike... and then he didn't come after all.'

'If you want Mike's respect you'll have to earn it,' Rachel told her bluntly. 'That man is the salt of the earth. He deserves the best, and so far he hasn't found it. Capers like tonight's won't endear you to him—not when an elderly lady gets hurt in the tomfoolery.'

'All right,' Felice said touchily. 'I've got the message...and I'll see you soon.'

It was three o'clock in the morning when Rachel heard a car pull up outside, and it was followed by the sound of footsteps on the terrace.

Toby had woken a few minutes previously, and she was rocking him in her arms in an effort to get him back to sleep. From the way he was nuzzling his mouth with his fist and from the bright red patches on his cheeks it was clear that his teeth were to blame for his wakefulness, and she thought that unless he dropped off again Felice wasn't going to get much sleep in what was left of the night.

When a key turned in the lock she was ready with a cool greeting for the thoughtless mother, but it was Nicholas who stood there, eyeing her in amazement as she appeared in the hallway with the baby in her arms.

For a fleeting second she saw a strange look in his eyes. If it had been anyone else but he she would have described it as wistful, but that wasn't the kind of word one would apply to him, was it?

'What's wrong?' he asked, immediately going straight to the heart of the matter.

'Meg has had an accident,' she told him with similar brevity. 'Felice is at the hospital with her.'

He frowned. 'I would have thought *you* would be more use there, while Felice minded her own child.'

Rachel stiffened. It seemed like a lifetime since she'd seen him, and his first words were bordering on censure. Maybe he didn't see her as the maternal type. Perhaps he could only visualise her with a stethoscope and a doctor's bag.

If that *was* the case there was no way that she was going to let him see that holding the small warm bundle that was his nephew in her arms was bringing back the yearning that was always there when she held a baby.

'Yes, maybe I would be more use at the Infirmary than Felice,' she said stiffly, 'but your sister insisted on going, and someone had to look after Toby.' She glanced down and saw that sleep had claimed him once more. 'I'll take him up to his cot and then, if it's all the same to you, I'll be off.'

'Not before you've told me what's happened to Meg,' he said in a low voice as they went up the stairs together.

Rachel eyed him warily. It was not her place to tell him what had gone on at his sister's party. Felice could do the explaining, and whether or not she would do it truthfully depended on how honest she was. 'Meg fell and broke her hip,' she told him briefly. 'Felice came for me when it happened and I sent for an ambulance, as I was pretty sure she'd sustained a fractured femur.'

'I see,' he said grimly and Rachel was sure that he didn't. He didn't see at all, but he soon would if Felice came clean.

As she laid the baby gently on the cot and covered him with a soft white quilt, Nicholas was eyeing her from the other side. When their eyes met he said, with an abruptness that startled her, 'Why have *you* never had children, Rachel?'

She looked away so that he wouldn't see the pain in her eyes. 'Two reasons,' she told him quietly. 'There never seemed the right moment to start a family. . .and Rob was so much like a child himself that I was afraid to risk it. When we split up it was a great relief to me that there were no young ones to be hurt.'

She swivelled back to face him. 'I've answered *your* question. Perhaps now you'll answer one of mine?'

'Fire away,' he said blandly.

'Why have *you* never married?'

There was an ironic gleam in his eye, as if the question was only what he had expected. 'That's soon answered. I've never found anybody that I want to wake up with for the next fifty years. Maybe I'm too hard to please.'

She turned away again. She'd asked for it. . .and got it. If there was one thing she could rely on with Nick Page it was a straight answer, and if he *was* hard to please he wasn't likely to want to throw in his lot with a washed-out divorcee.

Weariness and exhaustion bore down on her in that

moment, and as she made for the door of the nursery Rachel stumbled over a brightly coloured rug beside the cot.

His arms came out to steady her and as she righted herself he didn't remove them. She could feel the strength of his grip and his breath on her face, and the memory of when she'd been in his arms before came back so vividly that Rachel felt as if she couldn't breathe.

But she reminded herself that Nicholas had just made it clear that he was still searching for the right woman and, that being so, he was hardly likely to repeat his previous performance, yet it looked as if she was about to be proved wrong.

He was eyeing her lips as if he'd found an oasis in the desert and yet, as his arms tightened around her with a reassuring urgency, he murmured, 'You're so pale your skin looks transparent in this light, Rachel, and there isn't an ounce of spare flesh on you. Your bone structure is beautiful but I'd be happier to see it a little more covered.'

She stared at him. Was this his way of saying that she was skin and bone? And if it was he was right, wasn't he? After two weeks with the curvy Gaynor that was how she must look—and to think that she'd thought it was desire that she'd seen in his eyes.

Unable to bear the tension of waiting to see if he *was* going to take advantage of their disturbing nearness, Rachel slid out of his arms and made for the door once more and this time she didn't stumble.

As she went out into the velvet night she was aching for what could have been if only *she* wasn't so afraid of being hurt again and *he* so clinically minded. As she lay once more in the bed that she'd left so quickly an eternity ago, her last thoughts before fatigue claimed her were that she really must get a grip on herself.

The pain that Rob had caused her would seem as nothing compared to the hurt that could come from her new-found love for Nicholas if she didn't shut it out of her mind and heart. There could be no future in loving a man for whom the right woman hadn't yet been created and who held himself in such high esteem that no one was good enough, which was a far cry from her own battered ego.

Tomorrow was going to be the first day of a new resolve, she vowed as dawn began to brighten the sky—a resolve that was going to bring peace of mind and tranquillity, and if loneliness continued to be part of the package, so be it.

The following day was Saturday when there was just a morning surgery, and as part of her dawn resolutions Rachel had promised herself that she would catch up on her sleep during the weekend—if it was the last thing she did. The Page family were not going to exist for the next two days, and maybe by the time Monday dawned she would be feeling more resilient.

Mike's first words brought the previous night quickly back into focus, however. 'Felice hasn't turned up,' he informed her when, tired and heavy-eyed, she put in an appearance.

'I'm not surprised,' Rachel told him, and went on to relate the happenings that were responsible for the girl's absence.

When she'd finished Mike's face was sombre. 'She invited me round,' he informed her, 'but as Janice is watching everything I do at the moment, in an attempt to catch me out in a situation that might explain my recent behaviour, I refused as I feel that Felice is quite capable of messing up her own life without any help from me.'

'Well, she was doing that all right last night,' Rachel

said grimly, 'and Meg was the sufferer.'

'If I'd accepted the invitation it wouldn't have happened,' he said worriedly. 'I would never have let things get out of hand, nor would Nicholas if he'd been there. I'll call round at the hall after surgery to see how they're coping without Meg.'

'Nicholas arrived while I was minding Toby,' she told him, 'so Felice isn't completely alone there.'

'I'll call round, even so,' he persisted.

'What is it with you, Mike?' she asked peevishly, still jaded from lack of sleep. 'Can't you see that she's a spoilt young madam, who should be standing on her own two feet by now? If she's a walking disaster area it's her own fault!'

He gave his twinkly smile and her irritation disappeared. 'I suppose you think that I'm a walking disaster area too—where women are concerned—but, whether it is so or not, it's only since I met Felice Page that I've realised how little I cared for Janice.'

'And how much you're attracted to a selfish single mother?'

He smiled again and Rachel thought, as she did frequently, what an uncomplicated man he was. Why couldn't she fall in love with someone like Mike? she asked herself, not for the first time, but she already knew the answer.

Nicholas Page was the rare vintage to Mike's basic brew, and just one taste of it had made her realise that drink it she must or abstain for ever.

'There was a phone call from Springfield before you got here,' he said with a deliberate change of subject. 'Work is well under way to repair the damage, and they're estimating it will take about six weeks to complete it.'

'That's brilliant,' she said, as the trappings of her

working life came to the fore. 'It doesn't seem the same
without our daily visits there.'

'They're not entirely cancelled,' he informed her.
'Ethan tells me that the day-ward is running under full
steam again, and one of us is down for the clinic on
Monday.'

'I'll do it,' she offered. 'I've missed seeing Cassandra
and Gabriella, and it will be nice to have a word
with Rita.'

'Ah, yes, Rita,' he said thoughtfully. 'That will be
two receptionists we've lost in the last few weeks.'

'Not necessarily,' she said drily. 'Felice is contemplating bringing Toby to work with her.'

'Good,' he said immediately. 'The therapy of being
occupied here is working. If she's alone in the house
all day with just the little one she could start moping
again. We'll have to start a crèche.'

'I don't believe I'm hearing this,' she said, laughing
in spite of her irritation. 'Are you sure that you're not
taking patient care too seriously?'

'Felice qualifies as both patient and staff,' he pointed
out mildly, and on that pronouncement they each sorted
out their patients' notes and simultaneously called the
first of the sick and ailing of the day.

Rachel's first sufferer had been having post-operative
care in the small community hospital when she'd first
come to live and work in the village. She'd found Alex
McIntosh, a middle-aged turf accountant, isolated in a
small ward on the far side of the casualty department
with a severely infected incision from a stomach
operation.

The state of the infection had been such that the staff
at Springfield had been afraid of the spread of bacteria
to other parts of the hospital, in particular the small
operating theatre, and it had taken massive dosages
of antibiotics before he had been allowed out of the

sterile area to which he'd been banished.

He had been discharged the week before the fire and had come into the surgery to have the wound, which was now healing nicely, checked by either Mike or herself.

Once the last patient had gone Mike left for the hall, and Rachel was left to tidy up after the morning's work. She sighed as a footstep sounded outside on the tiled floor of the passage leading to the consulting-rooms.

The last thing she wanted to see was another patient at this hour. A quick lunch, a leisurely shower and bed were her plans for the afternoon, and she couldn't wait to put them into practice.

When she looked up the deep blue eyes observing her unsmilingly were not those of a patient, and for an uneasy moment she wished they were.

'Why didn't you tell me what had been going on last night?' Nicholas said, with his lean jaw tight and unrelenting.

'It wasn't for me to inform you about your sister's affairs,' she said levelly. 'I was only involved because I happened to be near at hand. If Mike had accepted her invitation to the party they wouldn't have needed me.'

'She invited Mike Drew?'

'Yes. I think he was the reason that she arranged it— as an excuse to get Mike on the premises.'

Nicholas was only half listening. 'You knew that Meg's accident was the result of her being manhandled by some drunken lout, and yet you didn't tell me!'

'It was for Felice to tell you,' she cried, stung by his tone, 'and, judging from the huff that you're in this morning, she has. Well, that is how it should be.' Her temper was rising. 'I'm getting tired of being embroiled in your family's affairs when I haven't asked for it!'

'Is that so?' he said silkily. 'Then we Pages will have

to keep out of your way, won't we? We don't want to be responsible for shattering the self-pitying cocoon that you've wrapped yourself in, do we?'

'How dare you poke fun at my life?' she snarled. 'If you're promising to keep away from me in future by all means do so! The less I see of you the better!'

Nicholas was smiling, but there was a tightness around his mouth which was making her nervous. As her eyes were fixed on his face she didn't see his arms reach out for her until she was clamped inside them. As his lips came down to meet hers he whispered, 'I never say goodbye to an acquaintance without some kind of farewell gesture.'

His kiss was hard and demanding, yet there was a savage sort of tenderness about it that made her bones melt and her heart twist in her breast. Then it was over as quickly as it had begun, as he put her from him and walked out of the surgery into the midday sun.

# CHAPTER SEVEN

THE small restaurant at Springfield was functioning again after the fire, and when Rachel went in there on the Monday for some lunch it was crowded with staff, day-patients and a good smattering of folk from the outside who came in for a well-cooked and reasonably priced midday meal at the community hospital.

The atmosphere was cheerful and neighbourly, almost like a club, she thought as she found herself a vacant table amongst the friendly diners.

It would have been sad if this place had been burnt down in the fire. It looked as if it was a meeting-place for young and old alike, who perhaps needed a chat and a bite with others to help the day along.

Ethan and Gabriella Lassiter waved from the queue at the self-service counter, and when Rachel looked up Bevan Marsland was coming to join her with a loaded tray.

There was a satisfying feeling of belonging and of usefulness to the community inside her at that moment, and she thought wistfully that if her private life was as clear-cut as her function in health care she would be totally happy.

Felice had turned up for morning surgery with Toby in his pushchair, and the captivating, dark-eyed baby behind Reception had provided their patients with unexpected 'in-house' entertainment.

Mike's pleasure as he'd witnessed their arrival had made Rachel even more uneasy about the attraction between the shy doctor and Nicholas's sister, but she'd thought wearily that she had enough problems of her

117

own on that score without becoming involved in anybody else's.

As she'd watched Felice performing the duties of motherhood and Reception with the quick efficiency she could produce when she felt like it, Nicholas's threat to alienate his family from her had seemed a vain one— with Felice in such close daily proximity. But it wasn't his sister he'd been referring to, was it?

When she'd asked Felice how Meg was she'd been told, 'Lucinda Beckman says she should make a complete recovery, thank goodness! Maybe now that the news is good Nick will calm down. He's been in a vile mood all weekend, except for when we went to see Meg.'

With the memory of their last encounter crystal clear in her mind, Rachel wasn't making any guesses as to what was bugging him but there was no way that *she* was going to start feeling guilty about it.

She understood his concern over Meg, knowing that he must have been appalled when he'd been told what had happened, but why he should have ranted at her for not telling him the full circumstances when he'd arrived home unexpectedly she really didn't know.

Would he have wanted *her* to greet him with the tidings that his sister had held a drunken party in his absence, during which a member of his household had been hurt? She didn't think so.

Her reasoning was interrupted by Felice, throwing a spanner into the works. 'I know Nick's mad at me for letting Meg get hurt,' she said glumly, 'but I also think that he's suffering from withdrawal symptoms.'

Rachel's heartbeat quickened. Had Felice guessed that there was something between them? But his sister's next words slowed her fluttering pulses.

'I think he's missing Gaynor. Two weeks continually in each other's company can create a strong bond, don't you think?' she'd said in all innocence, and Rachel had agreed weakly that she supposed it could.

Rita had been fitted for the orthopaedic corset and was up and about when Rachel went to see her before the start of the day clinic.

'How's it going?' she asked, as their plump receptionist moved carefully towards her.

'Not too bad,' she was informed. 'The corset isn't the most comfortable item of underwear I've ever worn, but I can walk all right now. The bed rest seems to have done the trick with the crushed vertebrae, and I'm going home at the weekend.'

'That's great,' Rachel enthused, sharing Rita's relief and pleasure, 'and I'm sure that they'll have told you to take care...no heavy lifting or climbing ladders.'

Rita shuddered. 'No need to worry on that score. I've no intention of doing a repeat performance. I just want to get back into my family routine...and return to my job.'

'Your job will be there when you're fit enough to come back,' Rachel assured her. 'If you don't believe me ask Mike, but he will say the same as I do...that we don't want you coming back too soon.'

'How is the new girl doing?' Rita asked, not entirely convinced.

'All right, but she's got a young baby and the nanny has had an accident. She had to bring the little one to work with her this morning.'

Rita goggled at her. 'A baby behind Reception!'

'Yes, a baby. We see enough of them in front of the glass, so I suppose an odd one behind it is permissible.'

'It sounds as if the sooner I'm back the better,' Rita muttered. 'I hope the child wasn't rummaging in my files.'

Rachel laughed. 'Toby isn't walking yet. He's not old enough to create any chaos.'

As she donned her white coat for the start of the day clinic Joan Jarvis appeared, with her own infant in her arms.

Rachel had only met her a couple of times—once on the night of the fashion show and again at the cricket match the following day—but she saw that Joan was making a beeline for her, and wondered if there was news about the cowman's son.

It seemed that there was, and it was good. 'Joe phoned from the Infirmary just before I came out,' she said. 'His son is out of danger, thank God! That poor man has hardly left the place since they took Sam in, and at last there is good news.'

Rachel smiled her relief. 'Yes, he's had an extremely worrying time but thankfully it's almost over, and if my information from those who are treating the boy is correct, there will be no permanent brain damage.'

The news had brought brightness to an average morning, and Rachel went about her duties with a lighter step. It was always difficult not to become too involved with one's patients, and when she was dealing with a sick child it was even harder.

His life had hung in the balance for the first twenty-four hours but a rapid intake of antibiotics had halted the infection, and the news that Joan Jarvis had brought fell happily on her ears.

In comparison to an illness of such seriousness, the first patient to present herself in the clinic seemed to be only mildly afflicted but Rachel was aware that her complaint was just as worrying to her as that of the cowman's son had been to his father.

Margaret Bryant had noticed that a mole on her neck was getting bigger and becoming flaky, and because minor surgery was not performed by her GP she had been passed on to Springfield to have it removed.

'I'll need to give you a local anaesthetic,' Rachel told the retired teacher, 'then I'll cut away the mole and a small area of tissue from around it, and send it away to be analysed.'

'Is it likely to be malignant, Doctor?' she asked bluntly once the mole had been removed.

'I can't pass an opinion on that,' Rachel said carefully, 'although I doubt any possibility of melanoma. If it should prove to be cancerous it is more likely to be basal cell carcinoma, which is the most common form of skin cancer and doesn't spread to other parts of the body, but the odds are that the tests will prove normal and it is just a harmless mole.'

When the clinic was over Rachel drove back to the surgery along leafy Cotswold lanes and, as always when she had a moment to herself, her mind turned to Nicholas.

He'd given her the chance to break free of him now. . .if she wanted to. That was the crunch. She *didn't* want to. She didn't want to be free of him at all. She wanted to be bound to him by a love that it was no use denying, and when she pulled up in front of the practice and saw his car parked outside she was out of her own vehicle in a flash—desperate to see him again, whether he wanted to see her or not.

He was perched on the corner of Mike's desk, a long leg swinging idly as he chatted to her partner, and Rachel was reminded of that first day they'd met. When she'd felt his magnetic pull and known that she was meeting a man whom she wasn't going to forget in a hurry.

And, yet, within seconds of thinking that she had been bridling in defence of the way she'd handled the patient he'd come to discuss—only to discover that he was there to praise, rather than complain.

'Hi, there,' he said, eyeing her trim figure in a sleeveless beige linen dress with a tight smile. 'I hope I'm not intruding.'

'No, of course not,' she said calmly. 'It's lovely to see you.'

'Really?' he said, as he almost slipped off the desk.

Mike was watching them in puzzlement. 'Am I missing something here?' he asked.

'No,' Rachel told him with continuing calmness, and went into her own room.

As she stopped to put her bag on the desk Nicholas was behind her, and as she turned swiftly they were chest to chest—the slender, brown-haired woman and the lean, charismatic man.

Rachel was willing him to take hold of her—longing to be in his embrace again, on whatever terms he chose—but his arms remained by his side and his eyes were cool and guarded as he said, 'I called in to give you both the news about Rita, but Mike tells me that you've just come back from Springfield so you'll be already aware that I've arranged for her to be discharged at the end of the week.'

She had herself in hand now. For one thing the surgery wasn't the place for raw emotions, and for another she didn't want to spoil it if Nicholas had given second thoughts to his angry promise of keeping out of her way.

'Yes, she told me,' she said levelly, 'and, needless to say, she's very happy to be going home, but she's concerned about her job here at the practice—thinks that she might lose it to Felice.'

She was watching him carefully. 'However, I've explained to her that the present arrangement is only temporary, and I left her feeling happier about the situation.'

Would he try to persuade them to keep Felice on? she wondered. After all, Nicholas—more than anyone, except perhaps Mike—must have seen a difference in the girl since she'd become occupied in something she enjoyed, and he must have also realised that Felice's attitude towards Toby had changed.

'Obviously Rita must be made to feel that her job is safe,' he said decisively, 'although it will be some weeks before I allow her to come back here.

'With regard to Felice, apart from that stupid, disastrous party last week, she has been a much happier person since coming to work for you both and once Meg is well again I shall suggest that she seeks further employment.'

He sighed, and there was a rare weariness in his eyes as he went on to say, 'If our delightful nanny can't, or doesn't, want to carry on looking after the little one, then we'll have to find someone else.'

'I wouldn't worry about that at the moment, if I were you,' Rachel said quietly, aware that for once she was in charge—that it wasn't Nicholas in command of the situation. 'You'll have a better idea of how fit and mobile Meg is going to be when she's discharged in a couple of weeks.'

'I suppose you're right,' he agreed, throwing off his momentary gloom. 'One thing is for sure—if she isn't completely active once more it won't be Lucinda Beckman's fault. That lady knows her stuff.'

'So I'm told,' she commented. 'She certainly always seems to have a heavy case load. Her post-operative patients come crowding into Springfield in their droves, new joints and suchlike being in huge demand.'

'Would you like to see *my* department?' he asked suddenly. 'I'd be pleased to show you round, if you're interested.'

'Yes. I would,' she said immediately.

He wasn't aware of it but she was interested in everything about him, and his job came high on the list. Not, perhaps, as high as what made him happy or what made him sad, or what his hopes and expectations were for the future. But, having finally admitted to herself that she loved this mercurial, clever man, she was ready to take any crumbs that were on offer. . .and, if she had to, turn them into a banquet.

'Perhaps one day next week, then?' Nicholas suggested. 'I'll sort something out and let you know. Obviously it will have to be at a time when we're both free.' He gave a dry smile. 'As long as you don't see it as another instance of my intruding into your life, it should be a rewarding time for us both. And now I must go, Rachel.'

He paused with his hand on the doorhandle and looked back at her. 'I almost forgot,' he said casually. 'You had a visitor to the lodge while you were out.'

'A visitor?'

'Yes. Male. Thirtyish. Blue eyes. Brown hair. Slight scar on left temple. Do those genetic details ring a bell?'

The photofit-type description would have been amusing if it hadn't been so easily identifiable, but she knew immediately to whom he was referring and there was nothing to laugh at in that.

'It would be my ex-husband,' she told him flatly.

'Were you expecting him?' he asked carefully.

'No, of course not,' she snapped, angry that Rob had tracked her down.

'Maybe he's having regrets?'

'I doubt it,' she said grimly.

'But you wish he were?'

'What kind of a person do you take me for?' she flared. 'Do you think I would go crawling back to him after being told I was no longer loved?'

'The man is obviously an idiot,' he said lightly.

Rachel eyed him sombrely. 'Nothing in the world can make a person feel more unlovable than to be rejected in that way.'

Nicholas walked back towards her and touched her cheek fleetingly, and her skin glowed at the contact. 'Yes, that may be true,' he agreed, his voice deepening, 'but it is also a fact that there is nothing to make one feel more happy and cherished than to be loved utterly and completely in return by the person one has given one's heart to.'

Stunned by this new side to the man she'd fallen in love with, Rachel blurted out the first thing that came into her head—and it was a far cry from what she was really thinking.

'You're obviously not speaking from experience, seeing that the woman good enough for *you* hasn't yet been conceived.'

For a moment his face went completely blank, and then fire sprang into his eyes. Turning on his heel, Nicholas headed for the door once more but this time it wasn't to go through it. He shut it firmly and strode back to where she stood, mesmerised.

'That's quite true,' he said calmly, 'but I'm working on it.'

Rachel took a step back as it dawned on her what he had in mind, but it was a futile move. He was pulling her to him in a manner that allowed no refusal, and then he was drawing the heart out of her with his kiss.

As she already knew, to her cost, his kisses were like everything else he did—a thorough, superior exercise. As their breaths mingled and her body warmed with the desire that he kindled so easily in her Rachel ached for more, but it was not to be.

Nicholas was breathing heavily as he let her go, and as she looked up at him with questioning eyes there was an expression of uncertainty on his face. It was so

unlike his usual countenance that *her* feeling of unfulfil-
ment was banished in the face of *his*.

But she knew that she must have imagined that there
was confusion in him when he said drily, 'I'm taking
samples, with a view to matrimony. All applications by
registered post with appropriate CV.'

'Get out,' she said wearily.

He shrugged. 'Sure. . .if that's what you want.'

'It is,' she said grimly and, realising that she had
never been more determined, he went.

For the next few days she was on edge in case Rob
called again but as time went by and there was no sign
of him she began to relax, telling herself that he must
have called that one time on impulse and had now
thought better of it.

A month later Rachel arrived at the surgery one morning
to find the area authority's monthly magazine, *Health
Line*, on her desk.

As she glanced down, glaring up at her on the front
page was the headline, TOP NEUROSURGEON VOTED
INFIRMARY'S DOCTOR OF THE YEAR, with a photograph
of Nicholas directly beneath it.

The article went on to say that the final vote had been
between Lucinda Beckman, the orthopaedic consultant,
and Nicholas, but the decision had been swayed by a
brilliant paper on brain surgery which Nicholas had
recently presented to the medical fraternity.

She swallowed hard. He was so on top of his job, so
full of drive and energy and yet his domestic life was
a shambles—with an unpredictable younger sister, an
elderly, now incapacitated nanny and a baby, all living
in a house that was far too big for them.

And as for his love life! That was peculiar in the
extreme. 'Big brother is very choosy,' Felice had said.
So, if the blonde goddess in Jersey hadn't come up to

scratch, was he really contemplating matrimony in such cold blood?

Yet there wasn't anything cold about his blood when he held her in his arms. It was always at fever pitch. . . and so was her own.

He was a very attractive man, while she was merely a pale-faced brunette, with huge hurt eyes and a detestation of betrayal. That being so, why did he have to use *her* as a base for his ego. . .for sampling, as he'd so cynically described it?

But, if his treatment of her was ungenerous, there was nothing like that in her pleasure with regard to the award. She was delighted for him that his skills and dedication were being recognised, and at the same time sorry for the very competent Dr Beckman.

'What about that, then?' Mike said, beaming at her from the doorway. 'Your admirer is justly acclaimed.'

Rachel felt her cheeks warming. 'He's not *my* admirer, Mike. I doubt if he's anybody's.'

'Really? Is that so?' he said innocently. 'Well, all I have to say to that is that before *you* joined the practice he'd only visited us once. . .and that was as a patient.'

She'd been about to point out smartly that Nick Page's frequent appearances at the surgery were due to the fact that Felice was working there, but Mike's last remark diverted her attention. 'A patient!' she exclaimed. 'And here am I thinking that he's invincible.'

'None of us are that, Rachel,' he said soberly, 'Nick Page included.'

'What was wrong with him?' she asked casually, one hundred per cent certain that it wouldn't be the common cold.

'Plenty,' he said, with deepening gravity.

Rachel felt the beginnings of alarm, but she took a grip on herself as Mike began to explain.

'The guy came to see me just after he moved into the area,' he said. 'Although I hadn't met up with him I was aware of his status, and was somewhat surprised to discover that he wanted to consult a humble GP.

'When he came into my consulting-room I realised that I knew him and it all came back to me as if it was yesterday, though, in truth, it had been six years since he'd been brought into Casualty after a car accident when I was doing a stint in a northern hospital.

'A careless mother had let her toddler run into the path of his car and, in avoiding the child, he'd crashed into a tree. The car caught fire and the police just managed to get him out before the whole thing went up in sheets of flame.

'He was brought to us with third-degree burns to the lower parts of the body. His other injuries were minor, but the burns certainly were not.

'I was in charge and we dealt with him in the prescribed manner, with painkillers and antibiotics, and treated him for shock with intravenous fluids through a vein in his arm. But almost immediately we had to transfer him to a special burns unit at another hospital, and it was with regard to the treatment he received there that Nick Page came to see me.'

Rachel was trying to take in what he was saying. 'What?' she gasped. 'Nick had previously been burnt, and yet he went into Springfield to get the old man!'

'Some guy, eh, Rachel?'

'Yes, indeed,' she breathed, 'but why did he come to see *you*?'

'He'd remembered me from all that time ago. When I discovered that his only immediate relative, who happened to be Felice, was abroad and couldn't be contacted, I started to visit him at the burns unit and we struck up an acquaintance.

'Though I must confess that when I'd heard about

the new fellow at the Infirmary his name hadn't rang any bells with *me*. I'd known at the time of the accident that he was a doctor, like myself, but as there was nothing professional in our acquaintance I hadn't been following his career or anything like that.'

'And?' she persisted.

'You want to know why he visited me as a patient, rather than to renew an old friendship?'

Rachel nodded.

'He wanted my opinion on the extensive skin grafting he'd had done over the years. Did I think it looked as horrendous as he did? As you are perhaps aware, Nick is a very fastidious person.'

She was staring at him, speechless. Nicholas Page was badly scarred, presumably on the parts of his body that he would least want to be unsightly. What a ghastly blight on his life.

'How awful!' she breathed.

Surely that wasn't the reason he'd never made a commitment with her own sex? she thought raggedly, but immediately cast the surmise aside.

Nicholas wouldn't feel that damaged tissue was anything to be embarrassed about. He was too down to earth for that, and any woman worth her salt would cherish a blemished body just as much as one which was unmarked. Rachel knew that *she* would, but chance would be a fine thing for that.

Mike was continuing. 'Most of the scarring was around the thighs and buttocks, and I recall him saying to me at the time—with his own brand of dry humour— that one of the reasons why he was always on the go was because there was no comfort in sitting down.

'This is just between us, Rachel,' he reminded her. 'Nick's consultation with me was completely confidential, and I wouldn't want to betray his trust.'

She nodded, turning away to hide her emotion and

telling herself that the chances of her ever seeing his scars was about as likely as Felice turning into the eternal earth mother.

Rachel had seen Nicholas only once in recent weeks, whizzing past the lodge in the blue Volvo on his way to the Infirmary—if the smart suit was anything to go by.

His offer of a visit to the neuro-unit hadn't been followed up, neither had he been near the surgery, nor at Springfield when she'd gone there. Short of booking herself into his clinic or banging on his door, there'd been no way she could contrive a meeting.

That had been the depressing part of recent days. The good part had been the news that Cassandra hadn't lost the baby. Since her collapse in Ethan's office after the fire she hadn't come back to Springfield. Bevan had been adamant that she rested and, knowing that she would be foolish not to do so, the senior sister had fallen in with her husband's wishes.

Even so, two weeks ago she had been admitted into the maternity unit at the Infirmary with a suspected miscarriage, but the news over the past weekend had been good—the enforced bed rest had cleared up the problem. The baby was intact and she would soon be home.

'She won't be going back to Springfield, I'm afraid,' Bevan had said, having imparted the good news to her when they'd met in the village post office, 'but once Cassie is home and back on her feet again she's going to have a farewell party at The Goose for all her friends. . .and that includes Mike and yourself, of course.'

'I will certainly come,' Rachel had told him, 'and I'm sure Mike will be there too. It's wonderful news about the baby. You've both had a very worrying time.'

He gave a tired smile. 'Yes, I think you could say that. Just as Mark is very precious to us, so is this unborn little one. We would be devastated if we lost it.'

'I'm sure you would,' Rachel had agreed gravely, knowing that there would be no lack of parental love for *this* baby, and she'd been ashamed of the envy she felt at their coming joy.

On the day after Mike's amazing revelations about Nicholas it transpired that *he* knocked on *her* door and when she saw him, standing there in the porch in a short-sleeved white shirt and denim shorts, her eyes immediately went to the lithe body inside them and they filled with foolish tears.

Being who he was, they didn't escape his notice and he said quickly, 'What's wrong, Rachel?'

She gulped the tears back. 'You're always asking me that! Nothing is wrong.'

It was true. Nothing *was* wrong. Finding him on her doorstep made everything *right*—whatever the reason for his presence. It was just that it was the first time she'd seen him since being told about the burns he'd suffered, and tenderness had overwhelmed her.

She wanted to take him in her arms and soothe away all his hurts. . .and she could just imagine how he would react to that! Nicholas would think she'd gone stark raving mad.

But she couldn't restrain herself completely. She *had* to touch him—to feel the cool, controlled strength of him—and, leaning forward, she took his face between her hands and kissed him gently on the mouth.

# CHAPTER EIGHT

NICHOLAS rocked with surprise at Rachel's impulsive action, but before he could either draw away—or take her up on the unexpected gesture—the slamming of a car door nearby made the decision for him.

As his attention was diverted from the soft lips on his he swivelled round, and Rachel saw Rob getting out of a smart estate car at her gate. She gave a gasp of dismay. What was *he* doing here? Why was he seeking her out? The last time they'd met had been just before the divorce and on that occasion he'd been so anxious to throw off what he saw as the chains of matrimony that she'd felt completely humiliated.

In the past she would never have hailed him as the world's most sensitive person but now, as he came breezing up the path and said chummily, 'Hi there, Rachel. How's things?' she could have hit him.

'Fine, thank you,' she said evenly.

'Not interrupting anything, am I?' he asked, with a quick glance at Nicholas's closed face.

Yes, you are! she wanted to shriek. Go back to where you've come from! But the last thing she wanted to do was start brawling with Rob in front of the man who, whether he knew it or not, had given her back a reason for living other than her job.

'No, you're not interrupting anything,' she told him in the same controlled voice. 'Let me introduce my neighbour, Nicholas Page.'

As the two men shook hands Rob said fatuously, 'Neighbour? There isn't another house for miles!'

Rachel pointed stiffly towards the winding drive that

led to the hall, but before she could explain Nicholas beat her to it.

'I live at Larksby Hall at the end of the drive,' he said with cold politeness. 'It isn't visible from this point, but you can see it quite clearly from the back of the lodge.'

'Mmm. I see,' her ex-husband said thoughtfully, but Nicholas wasn't prepared to be given the once-over by him and with a brisk nod he said, 'Nice to have met you, Maddox,' adding to Rachel, 'I must be on my way. What I came about will keep.' He then departed, long legs striding purposefully towards his own abode.

Rachel stepped back. 'You'd better come inside,' she said half-heartedly, 'and explain to what I owe the honour, as I don't recall any yearning for my company on your part the last time we met.'

Rob was looking around him. 'Quaint little place you've got here.'

'*I* like it,' she said drily, 'but you haven't answered my question.'

He slumped down onto her couch without being asked. Where at one time it wouldn't have bothered her now his easy familiarity irritated her, and she stood looking down on him unsmilingly.

'I came to tell you that I'm getting married again in four weeks' time,' he said casually.

A couple of months ago that item of news would have made her private life seem more inadequate than ever, but not now.

He was looking somewhat bemused. 'You're not bothered?'

'No. Why should I be? You've been making *your* preferences crystal clear for a long time now, and I'm not going to keep *my* life on hold any more.'

Rob wasn't to know that this show of positive thinking was a very recent thing and that the man who'd just

left was connected with it, but he was about to hazard
a guess.

'You mean you and this Page fellow?' he said with
a peeved note in his voice.

'No, I don't, Rob. I *mean* that you and I have nothing
left to say to each other. I wish you well in your new
marriage, although I have to say that I find it strange
that you're in such a hurry to shackle yourself again. I
think that was how you described our marriage, if I
remember rightly.'

'She's called Tracey,' he said sulkily, 'and she's
younger than I am.'

'Good for you,' she commented. 'That should work
out about right.'

'What do you mean by that?' he bridled.

Her smile was apologetic. 'Take no heed of me, Rob.
I really do wish you every happiness and now, if you
don't mind, I have to get to the surgery. My patients
will be waiting.'

He got to his feet. 'I see that nothing changes.'

'If you mean that I'm still a doctor. . .yes, I am, and
am likely to continue to be so.'

'There's another reason why I came,' he said awkwardly, not meeting her eyes.

'And what's that?'

'I wondered if you've any spare cash I could borrow.'

Her mouth dropped in surprise. 'What for? You had
your half-share of the house sale the same as I did.'

'Yes, I know, but Tracey wants a new house and a
big wedding.'

'So do most girls, but they don't always get it,' she
pointed out flatly.

'Yeah, I know,' he agreed, brushing aside the comment. 'So what about it, Rachel? Can you lend me a
few thousand?'

She shook her head in disbelief. Her ex-husband's

skin must have thickened to hippopotamus proportions for him to come up with a request like that.

'Most of my cash has gone into my partnership in the local practice and this place,' she said evenly, 'and it's left me with little to spare. I can lend you some, but it won't be thousands.'

Obviously expecting a rebuff, he brightened considerably. 'Great! Whatever you can spare.'

Rachel eyed him consideringly. Not so long ago she would have thought this the last straw and she supposed it was, but her life wasn't empty any longer.

She'd made new friends in a new place. . .and fallen in love. . .so it wasn't so hard to be generous, and as she walked to the gate to see him off it was as if a huge weight had been lifted from her shoulders.

'A kiss for old times' sake, eh, Rachel?' he wheedled, and because she was glad to see him go she didn't resist when he covered her mouth with his.

She'd meant it to be merely a peck but Rob, pleased at what he saw as his manipulation of her, had other ideas and he wouldn't let her go.

It was in the second before she realised what he was up to that she saw the blue Volvo streak past, with Nicholas at the wheel, and as it disappeared from sight Rachel thrust herself angrily out of his arms.

'You presume too much, Rob!' she said angrily. 'The fact that I've just lent you some money doesn't give you the right to do that!' Turning her back on him, she walked quickly up the path and slammed the door to behind her.

When Rob had gone Rachel paced distractedly up and down her sitting-room. Nicholas must have thought her a complete wet lettuce to be succumbing to her ex-husband's advances at such short notice.

No doubt he had also decided that she was extremely free and easy with her embraces, but if he did think that he couldn't be further from the truth, she thought rebelliously.

Yet who could blame him for making such an assumption? She'd kissed *him* the second she'd found him on her doorstep and then, only minutes later, he'd seen her in a meaningful embrace with Rob.

With her normal thought processes at a low ebb, she prepared to leave for the afternoon surgery. On her arrival she was told by Felice that Meg Jardine was due home that afternoon from her sister's, where she'd been recuperating, and that Nick had been in touch with a domestic agency and had hired a housekeeper.

'And where is Toby today?' Rachel asked, once she'd assimilated the two items of news.

'I've not given him away, if that's what you're thinking,' she said with pert defensiveness. 'He's in Mike's room. . .on his play mat. Mike said he would keep an eye on him while I get some filing done.' Sure enough, when Rachel peeped around the door there was Toby, gurgling with delight as her partner entertained him.

'What are you going to do about him when Meg is back at the hall again and the new housekeeper arrives?' Rachel asked curiously.

'I'll leave him with them,' Felice said. 'They should be able to cope, with two of them around. The housekeeper will take charge and Meg can do what she feels up to.' Her voice sobered. 'I won't be here for much longer, in any case, will I? Mike tells me that your receptionist can't wait to come back, and you won't want two of us around the place.'

'That is true,' Rachel agreed, 'but Nicholas won't let Rita come back yet—not until he's sure she is fully recovered, so you won't be going that soon.'

Felice perked up at that, leaving Rachel to marvel that a simple part-time job should mean so much to a girl of her background. That was if it *was* the job that was the attraction.

When Mike came out of his room at that moment, with the baby in his arms, she would have put her money on it being the boss rather than the employment which was making Felice want to stay.

On the following day there was no morning surgery, and Rachel went up to the hall with a small welcome-home gift for Meg. She'd seen Nicholas go past earlier on his way to the Infirmary, and once she'd satisfied herself that he wasn't going to be on the premises she'd set off up the winding drive.

It wasn't that she didn't want to see him—far from it. She longed to be near him again, but if he were to eye her with disdain—or make some kind of acerbic comment about what he'd seen between Rob and herself—she would want to curl up and die, and so she felt that the longer it was before they came face to face again the better.

In the last week Toby had become mobile, and Rachel found the elderly nanny watching him dotingly from a seat by the window as he shuffled around the room on his bottom, pausing every few seconds to observe them with laughing dark eyes that seemed to be saying, Look at me!

'Dr Maddox. How kind of you!' Meg exclaimed when Rachel presented her with a pretty box of toiletries.

'My pleasure,' she told Meg as a smart, middle-aged woman appeared with a tray of tea for them.

'That's Millie, the new housekeeper,' Felice said as she scooped Toby away from the occasional table on which the hot teapot was standing. 'I'll be able to get some golf in now that we have a full household.'

'Not so fast, Felice,' Nicholas's voice said from the

doorway and Rachel swung round, her eyes wide and startled.

'Hello there, Rachel,' he said coolly. 'I take it that you weren't expecting to see me, if your blank expression is anything to go by.'

A rosy flush was creeping up her cheeks. He'd read her mind and it was humiliating. Nicholas knew that she'd timed her visit to coincide with his absence, but something had brought him back.

'I have no clinics today,' he informed her briefly, still giving her the full benefit of his critical appraisal. 'In fact, I won't be at the Infirmary for the next ten days. I'm off to a medical conference in America— Chicago, to be exact—and I've just been to arrange the flights.'

His glance shifted briefly to his sister. 'So you see, Felice, we are still not going to be a complete household.' And you, Rachel, are not as smart as you thought you were, the look in his eyes seemed to say.

She was gathering her wits, determined that she wasn't going to look any more foolish in front of him than she already did. 'I see. I hope that you enjoy your stay.'

'Thanks,' he said abruptly. 'That is what I came to tell you yesterday—that my offer to show you around the neuro-unit will have to be put off for a couple of weeks.'

Disappointment slammed into her. So that was all he'd come for. Not to tell her that he needed her company as much as she needed his. He must have thought her a crazy fool when she'd kissed him, and what he'd thought of her when he'd seen her in Rob's too-firm embrace she daren't even begin to think.

'So, when are you going, Nick?' Felice asked glumly. 'And why have you left it so late to tell us?'

'Because I didn't know myself until yesterday,' he

said with a rueful smile. 'I'd intended giving it a miss, but that recent paper I came up with has got them intrigued over there and they insisted that I be included in the team that is going.'

Felice wasn't the only one who was feeling miserable, Rachel thought. She, herself, hadn't seen all that much of him in recent weeks but she'd known that he was near—that he was living in the big house behind the lodge, going each day to the Infirmary and calling in at the community hospital when there was a patient he wanted to see.

But during the next week and a half there would be none of that. It would be like it had been while he was in Jersey. . .deadly.

She got up to go, and it was clear that he intended to see her out. They paused outside on the terrace but there was silence between them. On her part because there were a thousand things she wanted to say and yet none of them were sayable. . .and on his because there was still a tightness about him, as if words were in short supply.

But not altogether, it seemed. 'Damn it, Rachel!' he said at last. 'How can you let that fellow you were married to maul you about like that? Have you no pride?'

Her throat closed up and she felt as if she was going to choke. So he *had* seen her in Rob's arms. But of course he had! He could hardly have missed it. They'd been in full view of anyone passing, and it *would* have to be Nicholas who'd been going by.

'Of course I have some pride!' she seethed when she found her voice. 'I thought that *you*, of all people, wouldn't pass judgement on me like that!'

'Like what?' he said through gritted teeth.

'Like somebody who thinks I'm easy come, easy go!'

He gave an angry snort. 'You frail-looking women

are all the same! You're beautiful. . .ethereal looking. . .as if a puff of wind would blow you away, but underneath you're hard, aren't you? A tease, who's not as fragile as she makes out.'

Her mouth was a round 'O' of umbrage as she listened to him.

'How dare you classify me in such a way!' she stormed. 'What is it with you? Jealousy?'

It would be music to her ears if it was, but this was more like a lecture. He could get lost, she decided. If he stayed in America a year it wouldn't be too long. Flinging herself down the steps of the terrace, she began to move quickly down the drive.

But his feet were pounding after her and, gripping her arm, he flung her round to face him. 'Not so fast!' he said with a dangerous light in his eyes. 'If you're so generous with your favours how about a little something to speed me on my way?'

Rachel tried to wrench herself out of his grasp but he was too strong for her and in the end she just stood there, his prisoner, with her eyes flashing and her chest heaving.

'What did you have in mind?' she breathed as his nearness made her head swim.

'This, for starters,' he said calmly and kissed her hard and passionately. 'And *this* for the main course,' he said in a softer voice and, cradling her to him, he explored the soft column of her throat with his lips. Then his hands were sliding down to her slender buttocks and his mouth moving to the smooth rise of her breasts. . .

In those moments of extreme pleasure Rachel was aware of a disquieting thought. Maybe he *was* jealous, and in his pique was using her to satisfy his own urges.

She wanted to be cherished, treated with tenderness, not lifted up one moment and knocked down the next.

With a finality that got through to Nicholas far more clearly than if she'd continued to struggle, she eased herself out of his hold and told him stonily, 'And *this* is for dessert. Goodbye, Nicholas!' As his face whitened she walked away from him—down the long drive and into her own small haven.

The satisfaction at having put him in his place lasted for about five minutes, and then misery set in. Why hadn't she told him why Rob had kissed her? That he was going out of her life for good, and what he'd witnessed was just a prolonged farewell on her ex-husband's part?

Why *did* she have to buy a house next to someone like Nicholas Page? she asked herself as she sat gazing pensively out onto her small back garden. Why couldn't her nearest neighbour have been a happily married man, or a crotchety old widower or a woman, for heaven's sake?

But, no, she had to find herself ensconced next to the most charismatic man she'd ever met, and with his charm went arrogance, hauteur and a brilliant mind—all ingredients that went to make up a dish that was too rich and unsettling for someone like herself.

'Get him out of your system!' the voice of reason cried, 'or you're never going to have a moment's peace of mind. This man might be the sort of person that dreams are made of, but sometimes there isn't all that much difference between a dream and a nightmare.'

Two things happened while Nicholas was away. The first was a cause for great relief. Springfield was back in full swing. The repairs to the small community hospital had been completed in record time, and on the day that the refurbished wards and subsidiary buildings came back into circulation there was great rejoicing on the part of Ethan Lassiter and his staff.

The second occurrence was unexpected and very illuminating. Felice came storming out of Mike's room one afternoon, with cheeks flaming and eyes bright with angry tears. Rachel eyed her in some surprise and wondered what her mild-mannered partner had done to upset their young receptionist to such a degree.

She'd grown fond of Nicholas's young sister, even though Felice could be a handful at times. She had decided that the girl had obviously been spoilt by their deceased parents and that fact, along with her astonishing attractiveness—*and* her role as an unmarried mother—was enough to create a personality problem in anybody.

'What's wrong, Felice?' she asked curiously. Mike wouldn't hurt a fly, but he'd obviously done something to upset Felice.

'Some friends of my father's in London are having a golden wedding anniversary party and Nick and I are invited, but as he's away I asked Mike to go with me.'

'And?'

She sniffled. 'He said no.'

Rachel smiled. Mike probably didn't see himself escorting the wilful young girl to a prestigious gathering of people he didn't know.

'Surely you've got lots of other male acquaintances you can ask?' she suggested tactfully.

'Yes, of course I have,' Felice snapped, 'but I wanted Mike to take me.'

When Rachel went in to consult Mike about a patient some time later he looked up with a wry smile and said, 'I've upset Felice.'

She smiled back. 'I'd say that was something of an understatement. She is both peeved and mortified.'

'Why, for heaven's sake?' he said, taking off his glasses and studying them carefully as if they held the answer to the problem. 'I'll bet she's got more men friends than I've had hot dinners.'

'It isn't them that she wants,' Rachel told him tactfully.

His head jerked up at that. 'Really? She prefers my company to that of the golf club lager louts?'

'It would appear so.'

'Yes, well, then, in that case I'll let her stew for a while.'

Rachel stared at him. Was this the easy-going man who had let the tight-mouthed Janice hook him like a fish on a line? As she pondered the matter he was answering her question, and her amazement increased.

'Do you remember telling me that when the real thing came I would know it?' he said.

'Yes,' she replied faintly.

'Well, it has come, Rachel. I'm in love with Felice Page, utterly and completely, but something tells me that I have to start the way that I mean to go on—that, with a girl like Felice, I could soon be submerged by her beauty and personality and there would be no joy for either of us in that.

'So, when she graciously informed me that she was prepared to allow *me* to take her to this up-market affair in London, I said no—that she could wait until she was asked. That in the circles I move in the man does the asking.' He sighed. 'And I'm afraid that it didn't go down too well.'

'You are brilliant,' she chortled. 'You've certainly sussed out the right way to handle Felice.'

He pulled a face. 'Hopefully. I shall now sit back and await results. In other words, I'll be hoping that I haven't blown it.'

It was Rachel's turn to be pensive. 'I wish big brother was as easy to manipulate.'

Mike beamed at her. 'So you and Nick *have* got

something going? I thought I hadn't mistaken the gleam in his eye.'

She sighed. 'If there *is* a gleam I haven't seen it. He thinks I'm the doormat type because he saw me kissing my ex-husband.'

There was a twinkle in her partner's eye as he pointed out, 'I think that's what Felice had me down for too, but—between us—we're going to show the Page family that they don't know everything.'

'*You* might be going to, but I doubt if I'll get the chance,' she said with unconscious wistfulness, and it was there that the discussion ended as the first patients were in the waiting-room and another session of health care was about to begin.

One of the first patients that Rachel treated in the now fully functioning operating theatre at Springfield was Harry Edwards, the gardener from the hall. The man had attended the surgery the previous week with a bulge in his upper abdomen between the navel and breast-bone.

It was very painful as it couldn't be pushed back, and she had informed him that he was suffering from an epigastric hernia which was going to need surgery.

'You mean I'm going to be in hospital, Doctor?' he'd said with gruff anxiety.

'No, Harry,' she'd told him. 'I'll do the operation as an out-patient at Springfield.'

He'd breathed a sigh of relief. 'So it's not that serious?'

'No, not really,' she'd assured him. 'There doesn't appear to be any underlying condition that's responsible for it, and so I'm expecting a straightforward correction of the problem.'

And now, today, he was waiting in the day-ward for her to perform one of the many minor miracles that

Springfield boasted of. She was going to give him an epidural anaesthetic, then the protruding intestine would be pushed back and the weakened area of muscle strengthened.

As she scrubbed up for the forthcoming operation Rachel saw the ambulance from the Infirmary arrive with its daily contingent of orthopaedic patients, and it went through her mind that the only consultant she hadn't met since arriving in the area was the famous Lucinda Beckman—she of the raven hair and autocratic manner, if what she'd been told was correct.

She'd make a good partner for Nicholas, she thought. Two bossy-boots together. With the thought of him the familiar ache came back—the longing to see him again and to touch him again, even if it meant crossing swords with him once more.

Cassie's farewell party took place that weekend. She and Bevan had arranged for a buffet meal at The Goose for friends and colleagues. As Rachel dressed for the occasion the melancholy which had nagged at her since Nicholas went to America lifted at the thought of an evening amongst her new friends.

A social life was what she lacked, she told herself as she braided her fine chestnut tresses into a coronet and secured it with a gold clasp. She had a wardrobe full of attractive clothes now but never seemed to have the opportunity or the inclination to wear them, and it was time she did.

Yet tonight was a casual affair. She didn't want to be over-dressed and so she chose a caramel-coloured suit that had a matching cream silk blouse.

As she inspected herself before leaving the lodge the mirror told her that the fresh air of the countryside and the slower lifestyle were suiting her. She no longer looked like a stick insect. Her curves had returned and there was healthy natural colour in her cheeks.

'You're making a comeback, Rachel,' she told herself, but the lost look in her eyes was a contradiction of the fact, and she knew that it wasn't going to disappear while Nicholas was pulling at her heartstrings.

The village pub was packed when she got there and as she looked around for Cassie and Bevan Rachel saw them chatting to Mike and the Lassiters.

She began to make her way towards them but was halted by a voice at her elbow saying, 'Hi there! You must be Rachel Maddox. . .the new GP.'

As she swivelled round Rachel saw a black-haired woman of a similar age to herself, observing her with long-lashed dark eyes. She had a striking face, with a strong mouth, high cheekbones and smooth olive skin, and as Rachel tried to place the person who had accosted her the stranger said, 'I'm Lucinda Beckman. You've no doubt heard of me.'

'Yes, of course I have,' Rachel said smilingly. 'Your name is a byword amongst the medical profession hereabouts *and* the staff and patients at Springfield.'

'That's gratifying to know,' Lucinda Beckman said with an elaborate sort of casualness which didn't quite conceal her gratification. 'The only snag to that is my job keeps me fully occupied and my social life suffers in the process. This is the first time I've donned the glad rags in weeks.'

The glad rags in question were a low-cut dress of flame-coloured silk and a black jacket with matching knee-high boots, making the dark-haired orthopaedic consultant look like a Spanish dancer.

What did Nicholas think of this rather overpowering woman? Rachel wondered. She had the confidence and style that would appeal to him *and* appeared to be unattached, but wasn't it supposed to be the attraction of opposites that held a marriage together? Or was that wishful thinking on her own part?

As the evening progressed Rachel kept finding herself next to Lucinda, and each time she observed the flamboyant doctor's brittle gaiety she thought that they were each seeking something—Lucinda, Nicholas and herself.

All three of them were fulfilled professionally, but that didn't fill the other side of the bed on a sleepless night or make each day's homecoming something to look forward to—instead of an exercise in loneliness.

Cassandra and Bevan, wrapped around with the magic of her pregnancy, were blessed because they had found that one person above all others to share their life with—as had Garbriella and Ethan, and Joan and Bill Jarvis. Maybe her concerns over Nicholas were a little premature. Perhaps he enjoyed being the strutting peacock who kept the secret of his damaged plumage to himself.

As they sat together at a table in the dining-room of The Goose Rachel saw that her companion was eyeing Bevan Marsland pensively and, to her astonishment, Lucinda said, 'That man doesn't like me one bit.'

'Who? Bevan?' she asked.

'Mmm, and I suppose I can't blame him. I once persuaded his brother to do something utterly stupid and he was killed. For years Bevan thought that Cassie was to blame, but she's forgiven me. *He* hasn't, though.'

'So you've known them for a long time?' Rachel said in continuing amazement.

'Yes,' Lucinda said flatly. 'Longer than I care to admit.' She pointed to where Cassandra's teenage son was playing a fruit machine with one of his friends. 'Bevan is Mark's uncle—not his father. The younger brother that I've been telling you about made Cassie pregnant, and she brought Mark up alone until Bevan came on the scene.'

'I didn't know that,' Rachel said slowly as it sank in. 'But what a delightful ending to a sad story—it's obvious they care deeply for each other.'

'Yes, they do,' the other woman agreed laconically, 'so maybe I'm to be partly forgiven for my misdeeds.'

Mike came over at that moment and as Lucinda drifted away he said with his quizzical smile, 'Felice is coming in later to have a drink with me.'

'So, is that all that's on offer at the moment?' she said laughingly.

His eyes twinkled at her through the lenses of his glasses. 'For the moment. . .yes.'

'She's a very lucky girl,' she told him, giving him an affectionate hug.

At that moment the door opened and Nicholas walked in. His eyes found her immediately, as if some sixth sense had told him where to look, and Rachel's arms fell away from her partner.

He was his usual elegant self, in a dark suit offset by a crisp white shirt, which made her think that he'd come straight from the airport. If that *was* the case she wondered why.

Had he fancied a drink before going home? Or maybe he'd known about tonight's affair before he'd gone to America. There was another reason why he might have stopped by, but it wasn't even worth considering. He wouldn't be as desperate to see *her* as she was to see *him*.

And, with regard to that, would the day ever dawn when he didn't find her embracing someone? she thought frustratedly. She, who lived like a nun. Who was just as choosy as he when it came to offering her affections.

As her treacherous senses kindled at the sight of him

she was telling herself that it didn't matter. He was
back. That was the main thing. But he was making no
attempt to come to her side. He just stood there, gazing
across with a dubious sort of frown, and it occurred to
her that nothing had changed. He still had his doubts
about her. Either that, or she was placing too high an
importance on her place in his life.

# CHAPTER NINE

BY THE end of the evening Rachel's feelings were a mixture of desolation and anger. After those first few moments of sombre scrutiny Nicholas had given her a brief nod and had then proceeded to spread himself around the assembled company in every direction but her own.

As he chatted to Lucinda she heard him tell the now-animated doctor that he'd just stopped by for a drink—that he hadn't known about the farewell party—and any hopes she'd had with regard to herself went by the board.

When she went out into the warm, starlit night just after midnight her intention was to pick up a taxi. There were always a couple of them cruising around to pick up late-night travellers, and it was with that thought in mind that she'd left her car at home.

'I hope you're not thinking of walking home alone,' Nicholas's voice said from behind her as she stood gazing up into the star-filled sky.

'Yes, why not?' she said coolly, knowing that much as she loved the peaceful village she wasn't so enamoured of it that she would walk along its dark lanes at this hour. But the desire to be perverse was strong within her, and once he had gone Nicholas would be no wiser as to whether she'd walked, hailed a taxi or flown over the fields on a broomstick.

But she was being too fast with her assumptions. 'You can either share a taxi with me,' he said snappily, 'or we walk home together. If you *were* thinking of walking home alone you want your head examining.'

150

'Oh, I need that all right,' she snapped back. 'Only a crazy woman would put up with *your* moods.'

'Moods!' he hooted. 'I don't have mood swings. I'm a reasonable man. . .and, talking about reasonable men, what about Mike Drew?'

'What about him?'

'I got the impression back there that he has Felice eating out of his hand. Seeing them was like a mirage. . . an oasis in the desert of my domestic turmoil. I would dearly love to see her happy and settled.'

If it had been anyone but Nicholas she would have said that he sounded forlorn, but she wasn't going to relent—not after the way he'd ignored her all night.

'Yes, well,' she said coldly, 'if you want to know the state of play you'd better consult Mike. I'm sure that you wouldn't want me to be gossiping about my partner.'

'I presume I must have said something in the past that warrants that comment,' he said, with equal frost, 'but I'm too jaded to go into it now. I've just had a long flight and have a pile of notes to unload when I get in.'

'Where's your luggage?' Rachel asked, aware that he was baggageless.

'I told the taxi that dropped me off at The Goose to take it up to the hall, but let's get back to what we were discussing. It's a beautiful night. . .shall we walk?'

'Yes, all right,' she told him tonelessly, 'as long as you're not going to collapse with exhaustion on the way.'

'If I do, who better to be on hand than my GP?' he said in a milder tone. 'But you needn't concern yourself. I'm not the collapsing type, though there have been times when I've wished I was.'

Such as when you were horribly burnt? she was tempted to say, so that he might know how she hurt for him. But she'd promised Mike not to break a confidence and, for another thing, her relationship with Nicholas was too clouded to touch on such personal matters, but how she wished it wasn't.

It was a night for lovers, Rachel thought as they strolled along the lanes leading to their separate residences. A huge silver moon hung in the sky, and small animals were going about their nocturnal scurrying in the hedgerows as they passed. But she and Nicholas weren't lovers, were they? They were a million miles away from it at that moment.

An owl hooted nearby and, startled, Rachel almost tripped over a tree root. Nicholas's hand came out to steady her, and as she felt the warmth of it on her bare arm she became still.

They'd been apart for ten days and now they were back together again, but in what context? Walking on the cold ashes of what she'd thought was going to be a mutually overwhelming attraction?

She'd told Rob that he presumed too much but she was guilty of the same fault, and she should have had more sense. Nicholas Page needed only to crook his finger and women would have come running, but because he'd paused for a temporary dalliance with her she'd thought that she was going to be the love of his life.

The supple fingers that guided the scalpel were still gripping her arm and, as she looked down on them he brought her from a state of cold logic to panic by saying levelly, 'I've been offered a post in the States.'

Her head flew up at that, and she strained to see his face in the moon's fitful light.

'And will you take it?' she asked, choking on the words.

'I don't know. It depends on various factors.'

'Such as?'

'Well, Felice and Toby, for one thing. If her life doesn't alter I would have to take them with me but, after seeing her with Mike tonight, maybe that wouldn't be necessary. What do *you* think?'

Rachel's heart clenched. He was asking her what she thought about Felice's and Mike's blossoming romance with regard to his taking up the post in America. He obviously didn't give a damn how it would affect *her*.

She was merely the convenient neighbour—not even classed as a friend, if his treatment of her in The Goose tonight was anything to go by. She was an outsider, and if she'd felt lonely before it was nothing to how she felt at this moment.

'I think you should do whatever makes you happiest,' she said quietly 'and only you know the answer to that.'

'That's not quite correct,' he said as his hand fell away from her arm. 'There's someone else that it could affect, and I'd want to know how *she* felt about it.'

Gaynor! she thought immediately. Or maybe he'd met some attractive American woman. She started to move away, desperate now to get home to the solitude of the lodge, but he caught her up and said angrily, 'Why is it that you are always so aloof with me, Rachel?'

That stopped her in her tracks. 'Me! Aloof with *you*!' she cried. 'The boot is on the other foot! You didn't even look at the side of the room I was on all the time we were in The Goose, and you accuse *me* of being aloof!'

He ignored her outburst, as if she hadn't spoken, and said in the same irritated voice, 'You were all over your ex-husband when he called to see you and tonight you were hugging Mike when I arrived, but if I even pass the time of day with you you're backing off.'

Her face was flaming in the scented night. 'You have a very short memory, Nicholas,' she told him stiffly.

'You were doing a lot more than passing the time of day the last time we met.'

'So you haven't forgotten?'

'Of course I haven't!' she flared.

Those moments when he'd pursued her down the drive and proceeded to turn her into pliant jelly were as clear in her mind as on the day it had happened, but what was all this leading up to?

On the face of it, Nicholas *did* seem to be jealous of Rob. . .and Mike, but he knew now where Mike's affections lay and so it was only the blustering Rob who was bugging him. Maybe this was the time to explain that her relationship with the man she'd been married to was as dead as the dodo.

'That day when Rob came it was to tell me that he's getting married again,' she said steadily, determined that she wasn't going to let Nicholas see how anxious she was for him to understand. 'When you saw us kissing by the gate it was his idea of a fond farewell.'

'And what was it to you?'

'The end of a chapter in my life.'

'And now you're ready to turn over the next page?'

His voice had deepened with an intensity that was making her tremble but there was no way that she was going to fall into any traps of her own making this time, and so she said blandly, 'I've done that already.'

'And?'

'It's blank.'

'It doesn't have to be,' he said, his voice deepening further. He took a step towards her and, without Rachel even being aware of it, her lips had parted and her eyes—glowing in the moon's light—were filled with a wordless invitation.

A car was coming towards them but so engrossed were they in each other that they were barely aware of it until Mike's voice called across, 'Can we give you folks a lift?' As Rachel dragged herself back to sanity she saw Felice, sitting beside him and shaking her head.

Nicholas saw it too and he said casually, 'No, thanks, Mike. We're enjoying the stroll.'

As his sister gave a satisfied smile her companion said, 'Fine. See you on Monday then, Rachel.'

She nodded absently, her mind still on the man standing next to her on the dark lane, but Mike and Felice had broken the spell and they walked the last mile in silence.

'I've got some words that will fill the blank page for you,' Nicholas said in a low voice when they reached her gate, 'but they can wait until tomorrow. . .when *you* might be more receptive and *I* less jet lagged.'

Her eyes met his, and hope was fighting with anguish in their hazel depths. The magic of the night and those spellbinding seconds on the lane before Mike and Felice had driven up would have been enough to send her to bed in a state of bliss under normal circumstances. But hanging over it all was the thought that Nicholas might take up the job offer in America—that he could disappear out of her life—and the pain of losing Rob would be as a mere pinprick compared to that.

'We aloof people take life as it comes,' she said quietly, and as she tilted her head to look up at him the long chestnut swathe of her hair swung gently on her shoulders. 'I can wait until tomorrow.' Before he could reply she'd turned her key in the lock and was closing the door behind her.

Thunder had been rumbling far away in the distance as they'd walked home, and an hour later the storm reached the village. Lying sleepless in her bed, Rachel watched the jagged flashes of lightning breaking up the night sky and shuddered as the thunder crashed immediately overhead.

Was it disturbing Toby? she wondered. And had

Mike got home safely before the elements started to run amok? She'd like to bet that Nicholas had crashed out the moment he'd got in the house.

'Aagh!' She gave a cry of fear. The room was filled with blue light, as if the electricity in the air had penetrated the house. The next second, as the thunder boomed forth with terrifying volume, there was a splintering crash and a creaking of timbers and as the ceiling came hurtling down onto her she saw that it had been ripped open by the huge branch of a tree.

Rachel tried to roll to one side to escape the falling debris but there was too much of it and, as something hit her head with a sickening thud, blackness descended and she knew no more.

When she surfaced there was pain inside her head, so much that she couldn't bear to open her eyes. She was aware that she was being moved, eased out from under a pile of rubble, and for the life of her she didn't know why it was there.

As she cried out with the pain Nicholas's voice penetrated her fluctuating consciousness. He was giving commands to those moving her in a voice that was as tense as a bowstring and—although the pain was awful—her fear went. *He* wouldn't let her die. . .he just wouldn't.

When she opened her eyes again one of the radiographers at the Infirmary was looking down at her and saying gently, 'We're going to X-ray your head, Rachel. We'll be as gentle as possible, but Mr Page wants it done from all angles and it could take us a good quarter of an hour.'

She nodded. It was too much trouble to talk and her head hurt too much. But where was he? Surely he was concerned enough to stay with her?

As if the other woman had read her thoughts she said, 'He's gone to get ready for Theatre so that no time is wasted when we have the plates ready for him.'

So Nicholas was pretty sure she was in big trouble, she thought bleakly. Maybe she *was* going to die and she'd never told him that she loved him.

'That was some storm out your way,' the radiographer said as she and her assistant took the X-rays. 'It's one of the snags of living in the country—there are so many huge trees that aren't as stable as they look. Quite a few came down last night in various parts of the area but the one beside your house that the lightning struck was the biggest, so I'm told.'

Rachel didn't answer. For one thing she couldn't remember a thing that had happened. It was news to her that a tree had fallen on to her cosy little lodge.

While she was waiting for the results of the X-rays a tall blur in theatre greens appeared in the cubicle where she was lying, and Nicholas's voice said from far off, 'Rachel! Can you hear me?'

She wanted to tell him that she could—that his voice was bliss to her ears—but she couldn't manage it. Darkness was descending again and as she slipped back into it the last thing she heard him say was, 'You're in *my* care. Remember that!'

A lifetime later she came back from the dark place where it was so easy to hide and found a young nurse hovering beside her bed.

'The patient is awake, Sister!' the girl said quickly as Rachel slowly opened her eyes, and with a rustle of crisp cotton the ward sister joined them.

'What happened to me?' Rachel asked weakly. 'I was in bed. . .there was a storm. The girl in X-Ray mentioned a tree, but I don't remember.'

'You will,' the sister said soothingly. 'You're suffering from pre-concussive amnesia. The blow to your head has blotted out all that happened just before it.'

'Where am I?' she asked weakly. 'The Infirmary?'

'Yes. You're in the neuro-unit. Mr Page operated on you in the early hours of this morning.'

'Oh, dear,' she whispered. 'He was so tired after travelling back from America.' She touched her head, where a section of her hair had been shaved off. 'And then to have this thrust upon him.'

The two nurses exchanged glances. 'He must have found a fresh burst of energy from somewhere,' the sister said. 'I've never seen him so poised for action in all the time I've worked with him. He didn't half give us all the run-around but, of course, you're his neighbour, aren't you? So it's not surprising that he wasn't going to let any more harm come to you than had already been done.'

Yes, she was his neighbour, Rachel thought tearfully. It was the only claim she had on him, but it didn't alter the fact that she'd been humbly grateful when she'd heard his voice back there in her shattered bedroom. . . supervising her rescue with his usual brisk competence.

'Mr Page will be coming to see you shortly,' the young nurse said as the sister was called away to the phone. 'He had you put in this small side-ward so that it would be quiet for you once you'd regained consciousness.'

'What exactly have I had done?' Rachel asked as she began to focus more clearly.

'The X-rays showed an open fracture of the skull, and he performed a craniotomy to repair damaged tissue and to drain away excess blood caused by the blow to the head. Also there were some small pieces of bone that needed to be taken out.

'Once that had been done the part of the skull that had been removed was replaced, and then membranes, muscle and skin were sewn back into place.'

She smiled. 'Obviously I wouldn't be giving all the gruesome details to a member of the public unless they were adamant but, as a doctor yourself, I imagine that you want to know all there is to know.'

'Yes, I do,' Rachel told her with a pale answering smile.

She drifted off to sleep again shortly after receiving the medication that Nicholas had ordered—antibiotics to prevent infection from fragments of bone and where wood particles had entered the skull—and when she awoke the day was well past.

'Has Nicholas Page been to see me while I've been asleep?' she asked the same young nurse as before, and was told that he hadn't. He'd left the hospital on some urgent business, but had kept in touch by phone with regard to her post-operative progress.

Rachel turned her aching head into the pillow. So she *had* been just another patient to him. Something more urgent was keeping him away from her bedside.

It was late evening when she roused, to find a man's figure standing by her bed in the dimly lit ward. For a second her world righted itself but it was Rob's voice that issued forth, asking sheepishly how she was feeling, and tears of weakness and misery stung her eyes.

'How did you find out that I was in here?' she asked listlessly.

'It was on the front page of the evening paper,' he said, shuffling his feet. 'WOMAN GP ESCAPES DEATH IN STORM HORROR. It said that the guy who is your neighbour heard the tree fall and, being first on the scene, he called the emergency services.

'Apparently, he lifted most of the beams off you himself, but wouldn't risk moving you until the paramedics came. When they arrived they found him shielding you with his own body from the overhanging tree which was about to topple into the room at any moment.'

Rachel was eyeing him with a wide, amazed stare. 'I didn't know anything about that!' she breathed. 'All I can remember is lying in bed with the storm overhead. I can recall nothing of what happened immediately before that. . .and afterwards I was only semi-conscious.'

'You mean you're suffering from amnesia?' he said uncomfortably. 'But you know who *I* am?'

'Well, of course I do,' she said faintly. 'It isn't that sort of memory loss. It's only the period before I received the blow to my head that's blank.'

Her mind was whirling and her confusion total. What Rob had just told her was incredible. Nicholas had saved her life, at great risk to himself, and *she'd* been feeling peeved because he hadn't been to see her.

Whatever lay between them, if anything, she owed him a great debt of gratitude, and the longing to see him became so intense that it barely registered when Rob said that he had to go as he was meeting his wife-to-be.

She managed to find a new stilted words of thanks for his making the effort to visit her, but the moment he had gone it was as if he didn't exist. All she could think of was Nicholas.

He came to see her at last and when he came it was night. The hospital was quiet. The night staff were going about their business with less urgency than that always evident during the daytime, and in the wards the patients tossed in their beds and mumbled their misgivings.

Rachel was thankful that she'd been put in a side-ward. Her head ached. She felt bruised all over and quite disorientated. So much for the cool, calm Dr Maddox, she thought wryly. The elements had brought her to the level of those she served, and if it hadn't been for a certain man she mightn't be here at all.

As she lay theorising the door of the room opened

suddenly and the night sister came in, with Nicholas close behind her.

Rachel's mouth was already dry, but it became positively parched when she saw him and waves of weakness swept over her.

She wanted to tell him how much it meant to her—his saving her life, not once but twice: the first time in her devastated bedroom, and the second on the operating table. The words stuck in her throat and all she managed was a feeble croak.

'Shush!' he said quietly. 'Don't exhaust yourself, Rachel.'

He examined her head with deft fingers, checked her eyes, her heart, and her pulse, and told her, 'You're doing fine. Complete rest is what you need now. No stress or over-activity. I can have you transferred to a private clinic in a few days' time, if you so desire.'

She'd been told not to speak and so she didn't reply, but it didn't stop her from making decisions. If Nicholas suggested a private clinic again she was going to tell him that just as he didn't have private patients so she was prepared to stay within the NHS during her convalescence.

As for avoiding stress! She was so tense that she felt as if just one wrong word would send her over the edge of sanity. For one thing, she wanted to know if there would be any lasting damage from the head injury she'd sustained and, for another, she was desperate to know just how much the disaster that had befallen her had affected Nicholas.

She was deeply grateful that he'd been there for her, and at the same time aware that she'd been wrong in thinking that he would have thrown himself into bed the moment he arrived back at the hall and slept the sleep of the weary traveller. He must have been awake like herself for him to have seen what was happening above the noise of the storm.

'Sister tells me that you can't remember anything that happened immediately prior to the tree falling onto your house,' he said briefly when he'd finished his examination.

Rachel nodded.

'Yes, well, don't concern yourself about that. It often happens after a head injury. The amnesia should be only temporary. By the time I see you tomorrow it might have all come back to you.'

'I hope so,' she croaked, with a feeling that there was something depressing hovering in her subconscious. Then, determined not to let him go without asking what was uppermost in her mind, she asked, 'Where have you been all day?'

Nicholas eyed her warily. 'Here and there.'

She closed her eyes. Whatever had possessed her to ask that? She sounded like a nagging wife *and* it was letting him see how much she'd wanted him to be there.

He touched her eyelids gently but his voice was crisp and impersonal as he said, 'Neither of us slept much last night. You need to catch up on your rest, Rachel.' He yawned. 'And so do I.' When she opened her eyes he'd gone.


The next morning life didn't seem quite so fraught. Some of the natural resilience that the body brings forth in such circumstances was surfacing, and she was prepared to be more philosophical about the catastrophe which had temporarily thrown her life into disarray.

She winced when she saw herself in the mirror. Her face was a mass of bruises and her hair, shorn down one side of her head, gave her a punkish look that made her vow to replace the long plait with a short stylish cut at the first opportunity.

Medically, Rachel wasn't sure how she felt. She still had no memory of events preceding the collapse of the ceiling, and told herself that an open skull fracture could be serious—not only at the time of surgery but afterwards.

However, apart from the memory loss she was experiencing, there was no other degree of disorientation and, having been operated on by the best when it came to neurosurgery, she was optimistic that she would soon be back in harness again.

Where she would live, she wasn't quite sure. Her vague recollection of the damage to the lodge was enough to tell her that it wasn't going to be a case of putting back a few slates and getting out a tin of paint.

There'd been a gaping hole above her as Nicholas and the paramedics had carefully eased her from underneath the debris. Major repairs would be urgently needed, but at that precise moment she couldn't be bothered to think about it.

Mike and the practice had to be considered. He was already making do with a stand-in receptionist and now his partner was incapacitated. He would have to find a locum, she thought sombrely, as there was no telling how soon Nicholas would discharge her.

He'd mentioned her going into a private clinic for convalescence, but she'd already worked out what she was going to do about that. She was going to tell him that she wanted to be admitted to Springfield for her post-operative care.

She had no family or friends nearby to take care of her. Although private health care was not to be sneezed at, if *he* wasn't prepared to be involved in it then neither was she.

For one thing, she would be isolated in a private hospital, especially if he was too busy to come to see her as he had been the previous day. Whereas at

Springfield there would be Ethan and Gabriella and the rest of the staff that she'd got to know.

But it was too soon to be making those sorts of plans, and as if to confirm that thought the door of her room opened and Mike came in.

Her eyes went to the clock. It was barely eight o'clock. He'd come to see her before surgery. . .before the day took its stranglehold on him.

'Rachel!' he said on an exclamation of relief when he saw that she was sitting up and taking notice. 'Thank God you're no worse! I would have been in yesterday but Nick wouldn't let anyone near you.' He gave his quizzical smile. 'He was guarding you like the crown jewels.'

Rachel managed a pale smile in return. 'Hardly that, Mike. I didn't see him after the operation until almost midnight. Almost twenty-four hours after the event.'

She was ashamed of herself for beefing about it, but it was still rankling. Her shame was about to increase.

'He may not have got round to visiting you but he was issuing forth his orders, nevertheless,' Mike said earnestly. 'If the nursing staff had reported anything about your post-operative condition which was causing alarm he would have been here quicker than the speed of light.'

'Oh, yes?' she retorted doubtfully.

'Yes,' Mike told her firmly. 'Do you know what he was doing yesterday when you thought you were being neglected?'

'No, I don't.'

'He was chasing various builders to get your roof shored up and immediate repairs under way, in between Theatre and his afternoon clinic, and when he did get someone on the job he stayed there until late to make sure that they'd made your house safe and weatherproof.'

There was no reproof in Mike's tone. He had too much respect for her for that, but she got the impression that he felt it was something that had to be said.

'I didn't know,' she breathed. 'I had no idea.'

'That's the way he is,' he said. 'Nick might appear demanding and autocratic on the surface but when he moves...he moves. He can't do with anything being left in a messy condition.'

The voice of the man he was describing came echoing back to her. 'Have you no pride?' he'd asked, after catching her in Rob's arms. What would he have classed that incident as? Untidy? Messy? Or just plain nauseating? Whatever he'd seen it as it had been the beginning of his withdrawal from their blossoming relationship.

She brought her mind back to practicalities with an effort and asked, 'What about the practice, Mike? You'll have to get a locum until I'm back in circulation again, won't you?'

'Sure will,' he agreed breezily, 'but don't you be fretting about that. I'll see who's on offer in the medical journals and, in the meantime, Felice and I will soldier on.'

He laughed. 'I'm thinking of putting an ad in the local papers, asking the population to do their best to stay healthy until my delightful partner returns.'

Her answering smile lacked warmth. 'Hardly delightful, after my moaning about Nicholas when he's been running all over the place on my account! Added to that, I look as if I've been in a rugby scrum and am suffering from a bad case of alopecia.'

He eyed her sympathetically. 'Your hair loss is due to a ghastly accident, not damage to the roots, stress or prolonged illness, and it will soon grow again.'

She sighed, aware that her earlier calmness had gone by the board. 'I thought my life was complicated enough before I came to practise here, but it's going from bad to worse.'

Mike patted her shoulder gently. 'Cheer up, Rachel. It can't be that bad if you've got the top neuro man running round in circles for you.'

'No, I suppose it can't,' she said with the same lack of conviction as before. As Mike got up to go it was there again—the desperate longing to see the man who seemed to be heaping coals of fire onto her shaved and aching head.

# CHAPTER TEN

THE next time Nicholas appeared he was carrying one of her overnight cases, and when she eyed it in surprise he said, 'I took the liberty of bringing you some clothes. I hope you don't mind my foraging in your wardrobe and chest of drawers, but as there was no one else to do it I packed some nightgowns, underwear, a robe, and a sweater and jeans for when you feel up to getting dressed.'

Her pale face had gone warm. He was sorting out everything for her. . .except her innermost feelings but, then, they weren't of any great interest to him, were they?

'That's very thoughtful of you,' she said with stilted gratitude. 'I'm not knocking the Infirmary's flannelette, but it will be nice to get into my own things again.'

She was pushing away the picture of his capable hands folding her lacy underwear and taking her nightgowns down from their hangers.

From the direction they were going that was the nearest he was going to get to viewing her lingerie. The chances of him seeing her in it were looking remote, to say the least, but there were other things niggling in her mind and the first one she brought forth was the one that was bothering her most.

'I still can't remember what happened before the tree fell,' she said with weary irritation, 'but I have the feeling that in the short period that is still blank something distressing occurred. I remember the first part of our walk home but the rest is just a blur.'

'It will come back, I promise you,' he said

167

confidently, as he read the chart clipped to the bottom of her bed. 'In the meantime. . .don't worry about it. Remember *I* was there and I don't recall anything happening to alarm you.'

Rachel sank back against the pillows, with the feeling that he of the straightforward approach was being evasive and when she felt stronger she would tackle him about it. Meanwhile she must be content to take each day as it came, and if Nicholas was there for some part of it that would be a bonus.

'Thanks for looking after my house,' she said quietly, as he checked her over. 'If you hadn't been here it would have had to be left in its damaged state until I was well. These are the times when one feels so alone. . .without parents, husband or children.'

He straightened up and looked her in the eye. 'You've me and mine up at the hall. We might be a nuisance at times but we do have our uses.'

Rachel had to laugh. He'd operated on her, arranged for her house repairs and even brought a change of clothes. Hardly a nuisance, but she knew what he meant. He was referring to the time when they'd crossed swords because she'd felt that he was intruding into her life too much. . .and now she couldn't get enough of him.

'Yes, you do have your uses,' she agreed. 'Without you, I would have been lost.' Her face sobered. 'In more ways than one.'

'Hmm,' he prevaricated, 'but you don't have to be too servile about it. By the way, as we are discussing my excellence, I hope that you have duly noted that I've contrived to get you the visit to the neuro-unit that I promised.'

Rachel made a wry face, and winced as the stitches in her head pulled with the movement. 'Yes, you have, although I would say that a very large tree should take the credit for that, rather than yourself.'

He smiled and it softened the taut lines of his face. 'Yes, I suppose you're right. It's strange that it took something like that to get you into my clutches.'

'I was in your clutches long before that,' she told him, and as she watched his dark brows rise she wished that she'd kept silent.

'Really? You'll have to tell me about it some time... when you've recovered enough to stand the strain.'

It was time to change the subject, she decided. She was in no fit state for personal discussions so she said casually, 'How are things with Mike and Felice? Any further developments?'

'Not that I've seen,' he replied, 'but, then, I've been very busy these last few days and still am for that matter, which means that I should be on my way.' His glance went to the case that he'd placed beside her locker. 'I'll ask one of the nurses to unpack your things and I'll see you tomorrow, Rachel.'

It was a week since Rachel had been admitted to the Infirmary and she was about to leave for Springfield at her own insistence as she was feeling much better.

The dizziness and disorientation following the craniotomy had lessened considerably, and a scan the previous day had shown that the operation had been successful. Nicholas had also been able to reassure her that the antibiotics had prevented any infection of the meninges.

'What about brain damage?' she'd asked. 'I still have some degree of dizziness and memory loss, although things are becoming clearer in my mind.'

For a second he'd dropped the mantle of the consultant and had eyed her quizzically. 'From what I've seen of you since I operated I'd say that your mental processes are in first-class working order.'

'Hardly!' she'd protested wryly. 'I don't seem to have had one straight thought since I came in here.'

His eyes had challenged her as he'd replied, 'That doesn't necessarily have anything to do with your injuries, does it?'

'You mean to say that my thought processes are normally confused?' she'd protested.

He was actually laughing—for the first time since she'd been brought in. The rest of the time he'd had an expression of such gravity that she'd wondered if he wasn't telling her the full story of her injuries or was playing down the damage to her house, which as yet she hadn't given much thought to.

But he became serious again almost immediately and told her crisply, 'It doesn't always follow that a depressed fracture of the skull causes brain damage, and in your case I don't think it has or will. For one thing, you were operated on promptly. The blood from the ruptured vessels was drained away and bone fragments hadn't been embedded in the brain to any great extent.

'The shape of your skull might have altered a little, but it shouldn't reduce your attractions.'

'Attractions!' she said glumly. 'With a face all the colours of the rainbow and a chunk of hair missing!'

He eyed her with smiling mockery. 'Yes, but don't they tell us that beauty is in the eye of the beholder?'

Rachel turned her face away. She'd never felt less desirable in her life and he was making light of it. But that was how it had been all the time she'd been on the neuro-unit. One moment he was the doctor, brisk and impersonal—his face closed against her. The next he was treating her with a sort of guarded friendliness, and that was why she'd asked to be passed on to Springfield for the next part of her recovery.

Nicholas had frowned when she'd made the request.

She'd already told him earlier in the week that she preferred the community hospital to private care and he'd had no objection, but when she'd suggested being transferred there he hadn't been exactly enthusiastic.

'What's the rush?' he'd wanted to know.

She could hardly have told him that it was agony to be in his care. . .but not in his heart, and so she'd said quietly, 'I'll be vacating a bed for someone who needs it more than I do.'

'All right,' he'd agreed touchily. 'I'll take you myself tomorrow afternoon, just as long as Ethan Lassiter can fit you in.'

There had been no problems with the nursing manager at Springfield and now she was waiting for Nicholas to take her.

The ward sister she'd met on that first day had been nearby when he'd asked her what the rush was, and when he had gone striding off she'd said with a smile, 'It sounds as if our Mr Page doesn't want to lose his favourite patient.'

'I would hardly call myself that,' Rachel had told her.

She'd laughed. 'Maybe you wouldn't but that's what *we* all call you. . . Nicholas's nut-brown maid.'

Now, as she waited for him, she was wondering what he really thought of her.

'Ready, are we?' he asked as he came through the door at that moment, pushing a wheelchair.

'Yes,' she said meekly, and with a sharp glance at her pale face he helped her into the chair, picked up her bag and they were off.

As they left the town behind and drove through the countryside that she had come to love so much Rachel gave a small sigh of pleasure. It was good to be out of the confines of the small ward, and as they drew near the village she said, 'At one time I thought I would never see all this again.' Or *you*, her heart cried.

He took his eyes off the road for a second and eyed her thoughtfully. 'But you were wrong?'

'Yes, I was wrong, and I owe it all to you.'

'My pleasure,' he said casually, and there it was again—the feeling that she was just like all the others to him. A sick body.

'Do you think we might stop by my house?' she asked, switching her thoughts to more mundane things.

'How much do you want to see it?' he asked warily.

'I'm not all that desperate, but I suppose I ought to be showing some interest in my property,' she told him. 'The problem is that I've felt as if I'm in some sort of limbo ever since the night of the storm, whereas under other circumstances I would have been frantic at the thought of losing my home.'

His hand left the steering-wheel for a brief moment and as he covered hers with it he said, 'You're not going to lose your house, Rachel. I have it all in hand but it is in rather a mess at this moment and I don't want seeing it to distress you so, if it's all the same to you, I suggest we give it a miss for today. OK?'

'Yes, of course, if that is what you think,' she said immediately, knowing that, compared to the loss of his interest, losing the lodge would be a minor catastrophe.

In any case, Nicholas had promised her that her home was safe, and she had cause to know that this man never said anything that he didn't mean.

Isobel Graham, the senior sister who had replaced Cassandra, was waiting for her when they arrived, and as she showed Rachel into a small side-ward she said with a smile, 'I feel as if I should say that I hope you will enjoy your stay with us, Dr Maddox, but I'm sure that, however pleasant we make it, you would rather be at home.'

'Not at the moment I wouldn't,' she said with equal friendliness. 'My house was damaged in the storm that caused my injuries, and at the moment it's un-inhabitable.'

'Oh, I see,' the other woman said. 'So I said the wrong thing?'

'Not really,' Rachel told her, acutely aware of Nicholas standing beside her like a guardian angel. 'It was a perfectly natural assumption.'

There was a huge vase of summer flowers in the room and magazines on the bedside table, and when the sister saw her eyeing them she said, 'Gabriella brought those in for you. She's off duty today but will be in to see you tomorrow.'

'That was very kind of her,' Rachel said gratefully. 'I'm looking forward to a chat with her.'

At least she could rely on Gabriella's friendship. With Nicholas, the future was too shrouded in uncertainty. He might be the confident human dynamo—the answer to the prayers of his patients, using his skills and dedication to give many of them back their lives—but when it came to his dealings with her she was for ever trying to guess what was in his mind.

'I want a word with Sister,' he said, unaware that she was conducting a character study on him, 'so we'll give you a few moments to settle in. All right?'

'Yes, of course,' she said immediately, and as they left the room she went to the window and looked out over the neat gardens to where the river surged power-fully over its rocky bed.

How long would she need to be here? she wondered. And what if her house still wasn't fit to live in when she was ready to be discharged? She would have to move into a hotel.

Nicholas was alone when he came back and when he found her still by the window he studied her gravely. 'Any problems?'

She wondered how he would react if she said yes.

That she had a big problem. . .and *he* was it. He would, no doubt, be suitably amazed. What was it he'd said that night in the starlit lane. . .that *he* didn't have mood swings; that he was a reasonable man.

Her eyes widened. It was coming back to her. The blank in her memory was being wiped away, and as it went she was remembering him saying something else. . .that he'd been offered a job in America. . .and when she'd asked if he was going to take it he'd told her that it depended on someone else. . .a woman!

'No. . .no problems,' she lied. 'My memory of events before the storm has just come back and—if my recollections are correct—*you're* the one with the problem.'

She saw him flinch and wondered why. 'Me! Why me?'

'The last time we spoke about something other than my health and the house, you told me that you'd been offered a job in America.'

'Yes, I believe I did.'

She had to ask, although it felt as if the words would stick in her throat. 'And have you made a decision?'

'Not about that. No. But there's plenty of time. They're going to hold it for six months. I've come to a decision about something else, though.'

Her heart sank. As far as she knew the only other thing he'd been contemplating was marriage. He'd told her so with a sort of humorous irony. Was *that* what he'd made up his mind about, and if it was then where, if at all, did she figure in the decision?

'And what might that be?' she asked, striving to keep her voice steady.

'You'll find out soon enough,' he told her levelly.

The room seemed suddenly full of shadows as her mind grappled with the implications of what he was saying, and at his next words it became even darker.

'You're still seeing him, aren't you, Rachel?' he questioned harshly.

Her eyes widened. 'Who?'

'Don't be dense! You know who I mean.'

'Rob? No, of course not!' she protested.

'He visited you at the Infirmary.'

'So?'

'So, the torch is still burning, from where I'm standing.'

'Rubbish!' she snapped, knowing that she wasn't handling this right, but on the heels of his other announcement it was just one thing too many to cope with.

'I've seen Rob twice since the divorce,' she said, her voice rising. 'The first time was when he called and you were there, and the second was when I'd just come round from the operation.

'He'd read about what had happened in the newspapers and, I imagine, felt duty-bound to visit me, especially as he'd just coaxed a loan out of me. If you've known about it all this time why have you only just mentioned it?'

'You weren't well enough to discuss it before,' he said flatly, and then went on relentlessly, 'You told me yourself that you hadn't wanted the marriage to end.'

'That's true. I didn't, but it wasn't because I still loved Rob. He'd killed all my affection with the way he'd behaved towards me but, ever optimistic, I didn't want to admit defeat, especially as I was the one who was surplus to requirements.'

Her voice broke. 'But why the inquisition, Nicholas? You've been giving me the benefit of your medical skills and looking after my house, and I've been deeply grateful. It has been wonderful to feel cared for. . .and yet all the time you've been judging me!

'There was a time when I thought that you and I

were made for each other, but I realise now that I was wrong. You keep your affairs close to your chest, but have no compunction in dragging mine into the light of day!

'I suppose you see *my* life as a mess compared to *your* well-organised existence, but it doesn't give you the right to be taking me to task over it. Even if I *was* still on intimate terms with Rob. . .what has it got to do with you?'

'If you don't know that I must be losing my grip,' he slammed back. 'Can't you see what's bugging me?'

As she eyed him mutely he opened his mouth to speak again, but she forestalled him by saying wearily, 'I'm tired. The transfer from the Infirmary has been more exhausting than I expected.'

It wasn't true. Any devastation on her part wasn't due to a short car ride and new surroundings. It was because the precious closeness that there had been between them of recent days had been wiped out by the conversation they'd just had.

In the last few moments he'd had ample opportunity to come straight out with it if he did care for her but, instead, he'd kept beefing on about Rob.

She'd told him that Rob was getting married again and that he'd borrowed money from her. Surely that was proof enough that there was no flame still burning, as he'd described it. There was no hankering inside her for what was past and, as if he was finally convinced, Nicholas took a step towards her. In the light from the window the look that she longed to see was in his eyes.

But only for a fleeting second. Rachel had her back to the hospital grounds, and as she watched Nicholas's face tighten she wasn't to know that Rob was breezing along the path outside, awkwardly carrying a bunch of flowers.

What she *did* know was that the special moment had

gone. Nicholas was looking at her with cold blue eyes, and it was only when the door opened and her ex-husband strolled in that she understood.

The man who held her heart bent over her, and his lips brushed her cheek like a butterfly's kiss. 'Get well soon, eh, Rachel?' he said with a complete absence of his usual zest, and as she nodded he went.

She awoke the next morning to find Gabriella beaming down on her, and as Rachel surveyed Ethan's beautiful young wife envy twisted inside her like a sharp knife.

The man who ran Springfield adored the carefree olive-skinned girl and Gabriella, in turn, worshipped her less zany husband. Rachel felt sure that one day, like Cassie and Bevan, they would have children, and when she thought about it the emptiness of her own life increased.

She was surrounded by happy marriages. So why hadn't she been able to make hers work? It couldn't have all been Rob's fault. Maybe if she'd had a nine-to-five job they would have been happier, but she hadn't flogged through the long years in medical school for the fun of it.

Medicine had been a vocation. It was what she'd always wanted to do from the time she'd been a small child, but Rob had never been able to come to terms with her devotion to health care—except for the occasions when it had been his health that she was caring about.

'Wakey-wakey!' Gabriella was saying with her bright smile. 'And how have you enjoyed your first night within these hallowed walls, Dr Maddox?'

Her momentary envy banished, Rachel gave a sleepy laugh. 'I've been as comfortable as could be expected, Nurse Lassiter.'

'And would ye be wantin' yer breakfast?' Gabriella asked with a servile curtsey.

'Mmm,' Rachel told her. 'What's on the menu?'

'Porridge and a Manx kipper for the rank and file, but for you ze egg and bacon, Doctair.'

As they laughed together Gabriella said impishly, 'We have a list of instructions a mile long from your dashing Mr Page. If he comes in to find you with as much as a sniffle our reputations will be in jeopardy.'

'Oh, yes,' she replied flatly. 'That's because he can't bear to lose a patient.'

'So it's not because he has yearnings for you?'

'No, I'm afraid not,' Rachel told her with a false show of nonchalance. 'The yearnings are all coming from my direction.'

Gabriella laughed. 'You could have kidded me, Rachel. That man has your welfare at heart. Have no doubts on that score.'

It wasn't her welfare that she was concerned about, though, was it? Anybody could deal with that. It was her bruised heart and unloved body that craved his attention, but that was crying for the moon from where *she* was sitting.

After butting in the previous day, Rob had only stayed a matter of minutes. He was on his way to be measured for his wedding suit, he'd told her, and as he'd had to pass the hospital he'd called in.

Rachel had eyed him morosely. It was typical that when she'd wanted him around he was never there, and now that she'd no use for him he kept appearing like some sort of irritating phantom.

'How did you know that I'd been transferred to Springfield?' she'd asked him listlessly.

'The local rag again,' he'd informed her. 'They've printed an update on your progress.'

'I see,' she'd told him, which had been true. There

*had* been a perfectly logical explanation for his presence, but Nicholas hadn't stayed long enough to hear it.

The time at Springfield went quickly in spite of each day's early start. Mike came in to see her every time he had to visit the hospital, and Felice brought Toby in one evening and told her that she and Mike had been to the cinema twice.

There was an uncharacteristic hesitancy about her as she imparted the news, and Rachel hid a smile. It looked as if her partner was still playing hard to get, and the amazing thing was that the attractive single mother was accepting it and not complaining.

Maybe the vastly different pair were going to make a go of it, she thought after the girl had gone, and the strange thing was that she didn't feel half as concerned to see Mike with Felice as she'd been to see him involved with Janice.

At least somebody's love life was getting off the ground, she thought glumly. Maybe if Nicholas took the American job she might get him out of her mind. He wouldn't be buzzing around the village as a constant reminder of what could have been and wasn't.

Cassandra called in to see her one afternoon, and Rachel was happy to see that with the averted miscarriage in the past she was now presenting the picture of the blooming expectant mother.

'What do you think of my replacement?' she asked as Isobel Graham passed the window of the ward.

'I like her,' Rachel said. 'She's very competent. A woman of few words, but when she does have something to say it is invariably worth listening to.'

'I'm glad you think so,' she said. 'Ethan needs all the backing he can get in the running of this place, and I was praying that whoever got my job would be a good choice.'

'I don't think you need have any worries on that score,' Rachel assured her. 'I'm told that Isobel is a widow with two children. She's bought a small house at the other end of the village.'

'Yes, that is so,' Cassandra confirmed. 'Stan and Olive, the elderly couple who have the post office, are her parents.'

'Really? So she's come back to where her roots are?'

'It would seem so,' Cassandra agreed, and after she'd gone Rachel thought that the only person around the place who was rootless was herself, and it didn't look as if there was going to be any change to that situation.

She could see the future mapped out for her. When the families of her new-found friends arrived she would become honorary aunt to Cassie's children and Ethan and Gabriella's offspring, getting the maternal fulfilment she craved from other people's babies.

Maybe she ought to get a cat...or a dog...and as the years went by she would be known as the reclusive GP at the lodge. Good at the job, but a failure when it came to personal relationships.

Perhaps Rob would breeze in one day with the brood that he'd never wanted when he'd been married to her, and occasionally someone might say, 'Do you remember Nicholas Page, the guy who was a neurosurgeon at the Infirmary at one time? He was over from America the other week with his wife and family as guest speaker at a conference in London.'

Rachel got to her feet. She wasn't going to get back in harness as quickly as she would like by wallowing in self-pity. A change of scene was called for and, going into the main ward, she told Gabriella, 'I'm going to take a short walk around the gardens.'

The young nurse eyed her thoughtfully. 'You're sure you're up to it, Rachel?'

'Yes, of course,' she assured her.

'All right, but the "force to be reckoned with" has phoned to say that he's calling to see you later, and he won't be too chuffed if you are not to be found.'

So Nicholas was coming to see her at last, she thought with quickening heartbeat, but her voice was casual enough as she told Gabriella, 'If I'm not there he'll have to come and look for me, won't he?'

'I don't think we need have any doubts on that score,' Gabriella told her smilingly as she halted the medicine trolley beside one of the beds.

Although it was a very warm day there was a pleasant breeze outside, and as she strolled slowly amongst the immaculate gardens of the community hospital Rachel saw an ambulance pull up on the forecourt and the paramedics on board brought out an injured man on a stretcher-trolley.

As they went past one of them said, 'Aren't you Dr Maddox, the GP who was hurt in the storm?'

'Er. . .yes. . .I am,' she admitted in some surprise.

'I was with the unit that got you out of the damaged room and took you to the Infirmary,' he said. 'Weren't you the lucky one to have a doctor on her doorstep? That guy was well and truly in charge while we were moving you. He made damn sure that you didn't come to any further harm.'

As his colleague pushed the man on the trolley towards the hospital entrance the chatty paramedic pointed to a small rose garden beside Out-patients and said, 'Talk of the devil! That's him, isn't it? Nicholas Page.'

It was indeed, and Nicholas wasn't alone. He was talking animatedly to Lucinda Beckman, and as Rachel heard her throaty laugh ring out she was fervently wishing that she'd stayed indoors.

'Yes, that is he,' she said casually, 'and he seems to

be in congenial company. Dr Beckman is another top consultant.'

There was an urgent need in her to change the subject—get away from the role of eavesdropper—and as the man turned to follow his colleague she strolled along beside him, putting distance between the couple in the rose garden and herself.

'What's wrong with the man on the stretcher?' she asked, for lack of something better to say.

'Industrial accident,' he said briefly. 'Works at the car firm just down the road. Had an argument with a piece of machinery and smashed the front of both legs. He's in a lot of pain.'

'Then it's fortunate that the orthopaedic genius is here,' she remarked. 'It sounds as if he's going to need Dr Beckman.'

It seemed as if Ethan Lassiter was thinking on the same lines as no sooner had the man been admitted than she saw Lucinda hurrying towards Casualty with her purposeful stride.

They must have bleeped her, Rachel thought, which meant that Nicholas was no longer occupied and could be on his way to visit her.

'Rachel!' his voice said suddenly from behind her. 'I see that you're taking advantage of a beautiful afternoon. How are you today?'

'Physically?' she questioned.

His glance was wary. 'Yes. Why? There aren't any mental problems, are there?'

'No. Not in the sense *you* mean,' she said recklessly. 'There have been times in recent weeks when my brain hasn't been functioning normally, but it has nothing to do with what happened in the storm.'

He was slitting his eyes against the sun's glare, and she couldn't see the expression in them as he asked, 'And what are the symptoms?'

She took a deep breath. In that moment of being with him again she knew what she had to do. After watching him with Lucinda, a desperate sort of madness had her in its grip and, although she might regret it to her dying day if Nicholas treated her with disdain, she had to say her piece.

'The symptoms are longings that I thought I would never have again. The aching of body and mind for a man that I've fallen in love with. The desire to care for him, to adore him and to be beside him for ever.

'Those are just a few of them, Nicholas,' she said, with her eyes awash with tears, 'but I'm not strong enough to cope with a rebuff. I hurt too much from what happened between Rob and I, and that is nothing to the agony it will be if *you* tell me that you don't want me.

'In fact, if you go away it might be the best thing, as far as I'm concerned. At least I'll be able to concentrate on my working life, even if the rest of it grinds to a standstill.'

He had swivelled to face her and, with the sun no longer on his face, she was able to see his reaction to her desperate confession. What she saw made hope spring to life in her breast.

'Rachel!' he breathed. 'So you *do* love me!'

There was wonder and, of all things, humility in his voice as he went on to say, 'When I told you I'd made a decision about something other than the American job, do you know what it was?'

'No,' she whispered. 'I made a guess, but couldn't cope with what I was surmising.'

His smile was tender. 'I'd decided that I was going to ask you to marry me. . .take my chances against the fellow you were once married to. You'd more or less convinced me that you might say yes, and then he appeared on the scene again and it was just once too often for me to believe that there wasn't anything between you.

'I'd been holding myself in check, waiting until you were stronger before I asked you to marry me. Surely you guessed how I felt? From the moment I saw you on the terrace that night when Toby was teething you've never been out of my mind.

'People see me as a very self-sufficient man and most of the time I am, but if you only knew how much meeting you has shaken my foundations—how much I've wanted to be a part of your life.

'I once told you that the woman for me hadn't been born, but I was fibbing. I knew that she had from the moment we met but there was an ex-husband who, to me, didn't seem as "ex" as I would have liked, and there was your reserve—keeping me at bay all the time.'

His voice deepened. 'When the roof fell in on you I nearly went insane. If you'd been killed there would have been nothing left for me but with a bit of assistance from myself. . .and God willing. . .you were spared, and yet my rejoicing was blighted with jealousy when your ex kept turning up.'

'There was no need, Nicholas,' she told him softly. 'Even if there had still been some small amount of feeling in me for Rob it would have disappeared when I met you.'

'Thank you for that,' he said huskily, 'but there is something you need to know before you commit yourself.' The light in his eyes wasn't so bright as it had been.

'I was in an accident some years back and was badly burnt around my thighs and buttocks. The scar tissue is not a pretty sight. *I* can cope with it, but what about *you*?'

They still hadn't touched. Several inches separated them but at his words she was across the divide, holding him to her and covering his face with kisses.

'We're both scarred, Nicholas,' she said gently. 'Mine are the rough weals of rejection...yours the result of what must have been years of pain and suffering.'

Her voice was tender. 'I already knew about your burns. Mike told me. You have no idea how many times I've longed to hold you in my arms and share your hurt, but I was afraid you would think I was presuming too much.'

'I can't believe that this is really happening,' he whispered with his lips against her hair. 'You've no idea how many sleepless nights I've spent, wondering whether you would ever be mine.

'In the last few moments I've glimpsed paradise... And, Rachel, I've seen you with Toby. I know how much you want a child, and I want you to know that my injuries didn't affect that part of my anatomy. I can give you all the children you want.'

'It wouldn't matter if you couldn't,' she told him firmly. 'I love *you*, Nicholas, not your sperm count. If we have babies it will be wonderful, but being with *you* is the thing that matters most to me.'

As she looked up at him, her hazel eyes brilliant with joy, he said, 'I don't know what I've done to deserve this.'

'How about saving my life twice in twenty-four hours, for starters,' she said laughingly, but there was no answering mirth in him.

'I was saving both our lives, Rachel,' he said sombrely, 'because if you had died it would have been the end of my life too. That's how much you mean to me. You *are* going to marry me, aren't you?'

'Of course I am,' she told him with a smile that was brighter than the summer sun. As his mouth came down on hers she murmured against his lips, 'I feel as if I've waited all my life for this.'

It was two months later. They had been married that morning in the village church, and when Rachel had seen the look in the eyes of the man waiting for her at the altar she had glowed back at him in supreme contentment.

Mike had given her away and Felice, radiant in her new-found happiness, had been her bridesmaid. Gabriella and Ethan had been there, as had Cassandra and Bevan, the Jarvis family and also, to her amazement, Rob and the busty young blonde who was the new Mrs Maddox.

Rachel had worn a dress of cream silk with matching shoes and handbag. A coronet of pale peach roses crowned the short silky bob that she had promised herself after the operation. Her pallor had gone and her smooth skin was faintly tanned from lazing in the sun during her convalescence.

When Nicholas had seen her the previous evening in the newly repaired lodge he'd said tenderly, 'You grow more beautiful with each day, Rachel.'

Secure in his love, she'd laughed up at him and teased, 'So I don't look like a stick insect any more?'

'You never did,' he'd assured her as his arms encircled her waist. 'You were more like a piece of fine porcelain, which might break if touched, when you first came here.'

'And what am I now?' she wanted to know.

'Someone that I'm no longer afraid to hold,' he'd told her huskily, 'because at last you belong to me.'

And now they were in an Italian hotel room overlooking Lake Maggiore, with the magical island of Isola Bella rising from the lake's clear waters.

In a few weeks' time they would fly out to the United
States to start a new life together. Mike had bought the
lodge for Felice and himself, and the locum he had
taken on during Rachel's absence had accepted a junior
partnership in the practice.

Meg was retiring to a cottage that Nicholas had found
for her, and the hall was in the process of being sold
at a very generous price to the local authority as a home
for unmarried mothers.

But all that was in the future. In a few moments she
would put on the jade satin dress that Nicholas had
bought for her and they would go downstairs to dine
on a lamplit terrace.

When they returned to their room, hand in hand, one
of the most precious moments of their lives would be
upon them. They would make love for the first time
and as they adored each other's bodies the effects of
their scars—mental and physical—would fade within
the sweet, healing magic of their love.

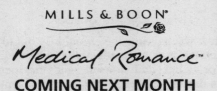

## MILLS & BOON®

*Medical Romance*™

# COMING NEXT MONTH

### NOT HUSBAND MATERIAL! by Caroline Anderson
*Audley Memorial Hospital*

Jill Craig was not impressed when the flirtatious, but very handsome Zach Samuels breezed into the Audley and proceeded to charm everyone—including herself! She could not deny the intense desire that they both felt, but could she trust him to love only her?

### A CAUTIOUS LOVING by Margaret O'Neill

Dr Thomas Brodie was reluctant to hire Miranda Gibbs. Why was such a beautiful, intelligent and diligent woman moving to the country? But then he saw her in action as a nurse. Miranda might get the job but she would never have his heart...

### WINGS OF SPIRIT by Meredith Webber
*Flying Doctors*

Christa Cassimatis had known station owner Andrew Walsh on a strictly professional basis for months, so she was astonished when Andrew suddenly proposed! She barely knew the man, and now he wanted to get married! She knew it must be for all the wrong reasons...

### PRESTON'S PRACTICE by Carol Wood

The name Preston Lynley rang alarm bells for Vanessa Perry! But then Preston provoked the most surprising reactions, including being incredibly attracted to him, from the minute she had begun her new job at his Medical Practice! But he also made Vanessa remember her tragic past—and his link to it...

New York Times bestselling author

# JAYNE ANN KRENTZ

## *Full Bloom*

Part bodyguard, part troubleshooter, Jacob Stone
had, over the years, pulled Emily out of countless
acts of rebellion against her domineering family.
Now he'd been summoned to rescue her from a
disastrous marriage. Emily didn't want his
protection—she needed his love. But did Jacob
need this new kind of trouble?

*"A master of the genre...nobody does it better!"*

—Romantic Times

**AVAILABLE IN PAPERBACK
FROM MAY 1997**